1

CYNIQUA MAREE

# MIDWEST CHRONICLES

## VOLUME 1

# CYNIQUA MAREE

WWW.CYNIQUAMAREE.COM

ISBN: 9781657787421

*This is a work of fiction. Any references or similarities to actual events, real people, living or dead, or to real locales are intended to give the novel a sense of reality. Any similarity in other names, characters, places, and incidents is extremely coincidental.*

# <u>Acknowledgments</u>
## Cyniqua Maree

First and foremost, I want to give honor to God who is the head of my life. Thank you, God for granting me with the ability to create. Thank you for giving me the strength to be able to write and finish this book. There were so many obstacles I was facing while writing and I want to thank you for leading me and guiding me the whole time. Thank you for giving me the strength to overcome everything that wasn't for my greater good. Thank you for giving me the words, knowledge, and mindset to share my gift with the world.

Thank you to my family and friends who are always so supportive, no matter what it is. I appreciate everybody that's in my circle and hope to one day be able to show my gratitude in an extreme way.

December 15, 2016, I participated in a short story challenge on Facebook. At that time my son was extremely sick and in the hospital. While being there with him I always tried to find things to help me cope with our current situation. I posted a short story that I created from a picture I found on the internet. I got such a great response; everybody was begging for more. That one short story turned into a 10-part series. *(yes, I included that short story in the book)* Every time I would post a new part. So many people would tell me I should write a book. Something that I only dreamed of; I had been good at writing since I was teenager. Fast forward to now and I want to thank each and every one of you who've been supportive of me from the beginning. I used that as motivation and here we are, my first book of short stories. Couldn't have done it without you.

# FAMILY OVER EVERYTHING

Once again here I am pulling up to the Milwaukee county jail to bail my little brother out. I was on my way from the salon heading to the nail shop when I got the call. He hadn't even called me yet, my homegirl that works there hit me up as soon as she saw them walk him in. Seems like the police are always harassing my brother Tank.

Another $1,200 down the drain, of course he was riding dirty and had some weed on him. The way things were these past couple of months, I wouldn't be surprised if he was clean this time and the cops planted the weed. Either way I wasn't letting my boy sit in there for no more than an hour before I was up there to bail him out.

"You didn't slip up and say shit did you bro?" I asked him as he was getting in the car. I love my brother to death, but he's a little wild and that's how he slips up at times. He needs to leave the drugs alone.

"Nah sis they weren't even on that with you, they were asking about pops" he said in a questioning tone. I looked at him like he was crazy. "POPS, our fucking dad?" Then he assured me that it was. Our dad's name was Big A. He's not our biological father he's our stepdad, but he raised us as his own and we loved him to death. He passed away about a year ago.

We always knew that Big A was well respected across the city and he had money, a lot of it. We lived in a nice house and him and my mom drove nice cars. Tank and I had a collection of nice clothes and shoes, he would even buy us designer clothes for family pictures or for our birthdays. Our mom worked from home, she was a party planner and worked mostly on the weekends. I had nothing bad to say about Big A, he was my hero.

When we were younger, we used to sneak around after Big A to see if we saw any clues about his job or work, but we never found anything. I always asked him where he worked, and his response was always the same. "I'm a businessman baby, that's all you need to know." When we got a little older, we started to understand more about what he did. He would show us investments that he'd made over the years, properties that he owned and a lot more. It's like once I turned 13 and Tank was 11, he was telling us more about what he did but still kept us wondering. Tank couldn't really comprehend everything while only being 11, but I was 13 and understood everything. Big A would tell us things like "trust your gut" and "don't talk to the police" and I always did whatever he told me to do.

As we got older, we didn't hear too much about it anymore. We took our own paths. I went to college for accounting after I graduated high school and started working at Saks Fifth Ave part time. I chose to stay close to home. Tank was an entrepreneur, most of his business was done the illegal way though. Big A knew what Tank was up to, but I never knew if he had a problem with it or not.

A couple of years ago, Big A got into a bad car accident where his truck flipped over multiple times. I get teary eyed every time I think about this, but it left him paralyzed. After the accident he wasn't his normal self at all, but I was happy he survived. The good thing about it was that he was still able to talk and make small arm movements. I remember when I got the call, I drove so fast to the hospital I almost crashed for crying so hard. It was a tough time for our family.

When Big A was discharged from the hospital a couple weeks later, he called a family meeting the day after. There was no way we were going to get used to seeing him in a wheelchair, but we had to deal with our new reality.

At the meeting it was me, my mom, Tank and our baby sister Leah, who was only 4 at the time. In the meeting, Big A explained to us that he thinks somebody close to him tried to kill him. He doesn't know who to trust so he changed his number and cut off everybody who he thinks could have been a part of the accident. Even if they didn't, he still couldn't trust anybody, we were the only ones.

"I can't move around like I used to, and I think this tragic accident is telling me to step back." He said trying to hold back tears. Never in my 21 years had I saw Big A cry. We all began to tear up, but continued to let him speak.

"I can't let everything I worked so hard for go down the drain just because muthafuckas are jealous. I taught everybody around me how to eat and it ain't my fault if they can't get off they ass and go get a bigger plate." He was getting really upset to where my mom had to get up and calm him down. I could not believe it even though I was seeing it with my own two eyes. My favorite person in the world was no longer that big strong man I grew to love, only a man who is now limited to his once everyday activities. I wasn't even sad anymore, I was angry, and I wanted revenge.

The more Big A talked to us the more he convinced us how serious this was, something we all already knew. He told us that I was officially over his operation. Everybody *must* answer to me, and I freaked out.

"Dad, you really think I can handle a responsibility like this?" I felt myself about to cry. I really didn't know if I wanted to cry tears of joy or cry of nervousness, or fear. I couldn't really explain it. There I was getting excited without even knowing what I was about to be doing. All I knew was that I was about to do whatever it was my dad needed me to do.

At the time I started thinking about the things he used to tell us when we were younger, and it dawned on me. Big A must be a drug dealer, I don't know anything about drugs though. I smoked weed occasionally, but I didn't like how it always made me sleepy. I didn't say anything I just put my head down and began to think. Just as I was about to decline his offer, Big A looked at me and I could see the compassion in his eyes.

"Tia, I understand this is shocking news, but I need you baby girl. I know you got this, I will teach you everything you need to know." I instantly felt comfort in his words.

"You can take this bigger than me, ain't that right baby" He looked at my mom. She agreed. I think my mom knows exactly what's going on, her and Big A weren't only married for over 10 years, but they were best friends for even longer. Everybody loved Big A & Tamela, they were like the power couple of the hood.

She looked at me and said "Baby girl we already have a plan on how everything is going to work out. You got this." She said to me while looking directly in my eyes.

"What about me" Tank blurted out. We all started to look around towards the floor like we just dropped something. We love Tank, but I wish he would make better decisions.

My dad said "Tank, I got you son" then we all pulled out pens and notebooks for us to take notes. We talked laughed, cried, brainstormed, argued, ordered pizza and had a good time. 4 hours had passed, and I think I learned everything I needed to know within that short time period.

Big A wasn't a drug dealer, he was bigger than a drug dealer he was an entrepreneur and had his hands in a few businesses. I learned that he was the building owner of the corner store we grew up around, it's still open and he upgrades it year after year. I always wondered why the store owner would never punish me and Tank for stealing when we were kids. Big A told us everybody who owed him money, owed him favors, who crossed him before, who he thinks will cross him. It was like a college course, Big A 101. He owned commercial properties, rented out homes and other real estate he owned. He was close to just about all the top drug dealers and hustlers in Milwaukee. We already knew that Big A was well known in the city, and now we see why. He was the reason behind a lot of people that's out here eating. He even had part ownership in other businesses as well.

Big A told us he lets one guy rent a property where drugs, guns, and other illegal things are sold. Nobody lives there but it's a nice house, they call it The Store. He told certain applicants to let him know if they plan on doing anything illegal in his properties. He was cool when it came to certain things because he respects everyone's hustle. He lets them know he charges about $500 more on the rent than he normally would, but its best that he knows what going on with his properties in case anything bad were to happen.

He has paperwork on everything he owns, contracts, I even saw a non-disclosure agreement in his files. I didn't get a chance to read it at that time but made a mental note to ask him about it later. While we were still in the meeting my dad texted me the combination to the safe, I figured he didn't want anyone else to know it.

In my mind I was already thinking this was going to be a lot of work, what was I going to do about school. My dad assured to me that it's okay for me to switch to part time or even take a semester off. I was already some credits ahead then average, because I was taking 5 classes each semester & 3 classes in the summer. Yes, I'm a book worm, and I think that's another reason why Big A wanted me in charge. I have the brain to do it.

After our meeting, I needed a minute to take it all in, so I split with my family and decided to go home. I had my own apartment on the north side.

Before I left my dad gave me a gun, a Glock 9 to be exact. When we were kids, he always took me and Tank to fields to practice shooting, and once we got older, we went to the shooting range with him. I knew how to shoot a gun, but I didn't own one. Until this very moment I never thought I would have to carry a gun. I had things like mace, a knife and a taser to protect myself, but not a gun.

One the way home I began to feel emotional, I could feel my hands shaking. I pulled over in the gas station to get my thoughts together. I couldn't believe how my life was about to change.

Less than a year after the accident my dad passed away. He died in his sleep is what the autopsy says, but he was so big on not trusting anybody but family. I wouldn't be surprised if his home nurse was paid to give him something that'll cause him to die. Nobody was to be trusted and I couldn't wait until we had proof.

The loss of Big A affected a lot of people's lives. Some showed genuine love but most of it was fake. My mom was a total wreck, so I had to be the one to step up even more than I already did within those few months. I was making me and my family money to survive and checking anybody who tried to get in the way. I kept everything professional and didn't let anybody get close to me, especially men.

The men in my city chased after me not only because of my smooth brown skin, small waist and thick thighs, but because I was Big A's daughter. I'm not sure if the streets knew he was only our stepdad, but that didn't matter. I was now one of the most powerful people in the city. Some respected it, some started hating, and worse of all people started thinking they could try me, and that's when things turned left, for them. No matter how old I was I had always been smart for my age and one thing about me, I was book *and* street smart. I built my own team of employees who I felt had my best interest. I never said too much around them so if something was to go down, I'll know exactly who it came from. Nico was my driver, and I had 2 bodyguards name Ex & Zo.

Now here we are my brother being scooped up by the cops, and instead of harassing him about me like they usually do, they're asking about our dad? I feel disrespected and need to get to the bottom of this. I know Big A didn't have this type of operation I had going on, but this is exactly what he wanted. For me to build an empire and create generational wealth for our family. I took his businesses, assets, and the money he left me to build even more businesses and more assets.

I was bringing in about $15,000 a week. A lot of people wouldn't even know that by just looking at me because I wasn't a flashy person. I drive a 2019 Jeep Grand Cherokee, but I was lowkey as fuck. All because I wasn't as legit as Big A. He wasn't 100% legit, he was more like 75%. I was about 50/50. Some legit hustles, some not, and some seasonal. I had money coming from every which way.

According to the police, it's rumors on the street about me saying that I participate in drug trafficking, human trafficking, and fraud. I wouldn't necessarily call it those exact things, but something close to it. Big A was still alive back when the feds started paperwork on us, and that's where all those rumors came from. I denied the fraud part to him at first, but eventually told him the truth.

By the time Big A found out about everything I had going on, I was already in too deep. I had girl hustlers and to me that isn't human trafficking. Milwaukee police are always trying to throw dirt on me and my family's name, and for a long time I never knew why. We weren't out here moving wild, that's how I knew nobody was to be trusted, it had to be somebody snitching.

I have homegirls that I manage that are strippers and they travel and get their money. Get Money Girls is what we call them. Nothing that they do is illegal. It's 6 of them, and they all have huge followings on social media. Some cities they go to dance, other cities they go to bartend or just get paid to host parties. Their bookings start off at $7,500 and goes up depending on distance, and the upfront fee isn't including the tips they'll make so they take home a little over 10 thousand each night they work, and I get 30%. I basically taught them how to make real money. It's been times where the girls would be traveling, and we would get pulled over. They would try to search the car but never had probable cause. Those racist cities are where the cops bothered us the most. Sometimes I feel like the feds were watching us closer than we thought. So far, we've had a clean run.

A couple of days passed since Tank got arrested. We were all trying to figure out the reason they even mentioned Big A. We never figured it out though. My dad's birthday was coming up, so we planned a family dinner in his honor, but anything my mother planned in honor of him was more like a party. It was his 50th birthday so this one hit us a little harder. The party was already planned before Tank got arrested and I wasn't sure if we invited anybody that was secretly a snake. Now I must pay attention to everything, and everybody then made a mental note to tell Ex & Zo to do the same thing.

We entered the party, and everything looked extravagant, we had so much food from fried chicken, lamb chops, greens, lobster tails, pasta, and so much more. We were planning on having a good time in remembrance of Big A.

The party started and no word from Tank, "He should have been here by now" I thought to myself, so I stepped outside the banquet hall and tried to facetime him. No answer. I called my cousin Blue to see if he was with him, no answer from Blue either. I was starting to get worried. Tank was one of those people who was always on time, no matter what else he had going on in his life he knew how to manage his time.

As I was walking back in the party, I saw Blues' car pull up. I felt a rush of relief thinking they've arrived, but when I saw the look on Blues face when he got out the car made me instantly know that something had gone wrong. He didn't even make it out of the car long enough before I rushed to him to see what was wrong.

"They got him" He said in a sad tone. "Oh, you mean he's arrested again. Let's go get him that's not a big deal you know how often this happens" I said jokily. "No Tia you need to listen to me, Tank was targeted, and I think he's dead" Blue said while bursting into tears. I stood there froze, I could not move for the life of me.

Then Blue goes to say, "He was on his way here when he got in a small finder bender, got out of the car and they sprayed him over 20 times" I still stood there froze, I couldn't make a sound. He continues. "I couldn't even go to the scene I came straight here, I wouldn't have been able to handle it." At that point I was already on the ground crying hysterically. I couldn't believe what I was hearing, my little brother just gone that quick. We left the party and let the guests stay, I didn't want anybody to panic until we figured out all the info. I told my mom we needed to leave asap but didn't tell her why right away.

Blue was driving me, my mom, grandma, and sister Leah to the hospital. Blue got a phone call and when he said it was Joe, one of Tanks friends, I snatched the phone.

"What happened to my brother Joe" I said in a calmer tone. I was starting to keep my cool because I knew I needed answers and crying wasn't going to help me. I had a feeling in the back of my mind everything was going to be okay. Whenever I have that feeling, I like to think that its Big A watching over and guiding me.

"Niggas is saying that fed nigga who been chasing yall all these years had something to do with it" he yelled. "What fed nigga? Hobbs?" I asked him. "No not him, his old partner" he said.

"The one who used to have beef with Big A too" I tried to think who. And when I thought of who he could be talking about, I became sick to my stomach.

"Don't tell me you're talking about Will"
"Yep" he replied.

I told Blue to pull the car over because I had to puke. That is when all my emotions started to come out once again. Everybody got out of the car to see if I was alright. I had to think if I wanted to tell them the news right now or wait. Thinking of my brother Tank with bullets all through his body is something we are not going to be able to handle, I might as well tell them now.

"Joe just said that it was a set up accident and Officer Will is the one responsible for the hit" I looked right at my mother who began to break down. Will was our real father.

I really hope and pray that Will wasn't responsible for what just happened. Tank and I were slowly getting to know him, me mostly because Tank didn't care to have a relationship with him. All of this was behind my mother's back because she told us to stay away from him and that Big A was our father.

I found out Big A wasn't our real dad when I was 14. I found my birth certificate in my mom's closet when I was looking for something. I didn't say anything to anyone after I saw it, I just went in my room and cried myself to sleep. I assumed me and Tank had the same father, but I didn't say anything to him about it either. I wanted to approach my mom so bad, but I never did.

Things went back to normal shortly after that because I couldn't build up the courage to say anything. After a while I just forgot about it and figured it was a real reason we didn't know. Big A ended up telling me when I turned 18. I told him I already knew, and he wasn't surprised.

"You're so smart for your age, you're going to be great one day" He would always tell me that. He also told me not to say anything to my mom, for some reason she wanted to forget our real father ever existed.

Whenever he would talk about telling me and Tank the truth, she would flip. Eventually Tank found out as well, he took it lightly. Big A was our father, no matter what. At the time he told me he wasn't our real father, he gave me a little information on my birth father. Said his name was Will and that he was a police officer. He told me that him and Will knew each other from the hood and they never really got along. Especially once he got with my mom and started to take care of us. Even though Big A didn't care for Will, he said he would get his information for me if I wanted to meet him or reach out.

"What exactly would I be meeting him for, you're my dad" I told Big A. After that conversation, we never spoke about Will again.

A couple of years later I decided I wanted to reach out to my real father. I thought to myself, how are you going to protect and serve everybody else but not your own. I wrote him a brief letter and had it sent to his last known address and told him to meet up with me if he cared to even want to know me.

Before I met up with him, I had one of my homies investigate his background, and found out a little about him. He wasn't married, didn't have any other kids, he was a low-profile kind of guy. That had me thinking he probably did a lot of undercover work as a police officer. I wanted Tank to meet him too but wasn't sure on how I would ask him. I decided to say something at the last minute, so he'd be forced to come. I pulled up to my mom's house, Tank was still living there at the time.

"Hey Tank, come out to all you can eat crab legs with me" I walked into his room while he was watching the game.

"I'm cool sis, I got some plans already we can go this weekend though" he said. That boy loved crab legs so I just knew he would come.

"Okay that's cool, guess I'll go by myself" I walked out the house and to my car. I was planning to meet with our real father tomorrow, I was going to tell Tank about it tonight. He always told me to forget about our real father and he doesn't care about him. He used to sound just like our mom.

I wanted to know who my real father was and possibly get to know him. I didn't hold any grudges against him either. Tank and I didn't know the relationship he had with our mom. Of course, I was more levelheaded about the situation than Tank was, because he never wanted to talk about it.

Will texted me and told me to meet him at Benihana at 6pm. I didn't want him thinking he owed me anything, but I wasn't going to decline his offer because I loved that restaurant.

I decided to dress a little more casual, not too dressy because I also didn't want him thinking he was special. He stood up when he saw me walking towards his table.

"Hey Tia Marie, I'm Will. You are so beautiful, and you look just like your mother when she was your age" He extended his hand for a handshake, but something told me to simply give him a hug.

My mom was the only one that would call me Tia Marie, I wanted to feel some type of way, but I felt his aura as soon as I got close to him and it was welcoming. I did sense that he had dark clouds hovering over him though. One thing about me is I was spiritually deep, and I could sense a bad vibe from a mile away.

Will took a deep breath while we hugged, and I could tell he was just as nervous as I was. Something about him was in tune with me, he *felt* like my father and it was an indescribable feeling.

We ordered off the menu and we began to ask each other questions. I thought it was going to be more of him asking me questions, but it wasn't. When I asked him about his job, he started to get tense, maybe his job was a trigger or something. I didn't let him know I noticed it, I just looked at him and waited for him to answer. I already knew he was a cop turned fed, and I knew about how he didn't get along with Big A.

He hesitated at first, then goes to say, "Tia I know we've just met, but I feel as if I already knew you." His began to look me in my eyes.

"I'm not sure if you feel the same way and that's okay but I wouldn't be able to live with myself if I didn't tell you this." I started to grow an attitude, he better not say anything that was going to make this his first- and last-time meeting with me.

"I'm a police officer and I got a new partner about 4 months ago. He's been building a case on your family, targeting your other dad Anthony" I looked at him confused when he said dad, we hadn't discussed Big A at all this whole conversation but the fact he referred to him as my dad let me know he respected the man who took care of his children. I didn't know what to say after that statement, so I stayed quiet.

"The moment I saw you were involved, I distanced myself from my partner until I was able to get a new one." I still didn't speak, just continued to give him a blank stare. Here I am meeting with my biological father for the first time, and he wants to talk about how his "partner" is trying to jeopardize my operation. Interesting.

"Tia, this is serious. My partner wanted to know why I was so nonchalant about the case. I never had a direct answer. He doesn't know that you all are my biological children, plus me and your mother never married we were just engaged."

I could tell that Will could sense the attitude and curiosity by my facial expressions, but he just earned some respect from me. Will seemed like he was solid, because he actually could have kept that information away from me, but he didn't. Or was he playing me? First impression last impression was all I could think of.

Me, my mom, Duke and my grandmother rushed into the hospital to try to find my brother Tank. The receptionist said they didn't have anybody by the name of Tank. My cousin Blue yelled, "He's the one that got shot on Sherman Blvd, he was inside a black Chevy Tahoe." She replied, "Yes I'm familiar with this case, his family is over there maybe they can tell you more information. Tank Harris isn't in our system.

I looked over in the waiting area and saw an older lady in her mid-fifties and a man about the same age, consoling each other. As I was about to walk over to them, I saw a lady rush in the doors and run over to them.

"What happened to my baby" the lady shouted, then I became confused, but it hit me shortly after. My brother isn't the one who got shot that was somebody else. That was the kind of truck he had though, I thought to myself.

"Blue who told you it was Tank that was shot" I turned to my cousin ready to slap the tears off his face. He looked up, confused. I rushed everybody back to the car. Blue pulled out his phone to check his call log.

"I don't have this number saved but it looked familiar that's why I answered" he said. "Whose number Duke?? You about to piss me off" I yelled so loud that I startled everybody in the car.

"It was a nigga like, aye man your boy Tank just got sprayed on Sherman Blvd" he said slowly. "I rode pass and the police had it sewed up, ambulance, fire trucks all that. I didn't get out to see if it was him, I came straight to the party to tell yall."

A feeling of relief came across everybody in the car when we realized Tank wasn't the one who got shot. Blue was about to drive off until I realized something, I knew that lady that came in. And that older couple looked really familiar too. That was the family of Tanks friend Cam.

"Damn" I said out loud. Everyone looked at me waiting to speak again. "Park the car Blue, that's Cam's mother and grandparents in the lobby" I told him, then I heard my mother start to cry again. Cam was the one who got shot, not Tank, he must have been driving Tanks car. My mom pulled out her phone to call Tank, but he still didn't answer.

I went back in the emergency room and approached Cam's mom. She looked up at me and began to cry, "Tia, what happened to my boy. They saying he got shot multiple times while driving, but his car is still at home" she said in between sobs.

"My parents say he's in surgery now, they're trying to save to his life" I grabbed her by the hand and sat next to her. I reached in my purse and grabbed the $2,000 I had wrapped in a rubber band and gave it to her while no one was looking. She looked at the money then looked up at me.

"Ms. K we're going to find out what's going on. In the meantime, if the cops start to question you don't mention none of Cams' business dealings. I promise you we'll get to the bottom of this" I gave her a hug and walked back to the car. I made a few phone calls to put some things in motion, I really hate that this happened.

We were headed back to the party, still no word from Tank. My mom was still so worried, and she was silent the whole time. I couldn't believe Blue ran with that false ass information, but Cam being shot is just as bad as Tank being shot.

The only thing that added up about this situation was that it was a set up, and those bullets were made for Tank instead of his best friend. It was Tanks car he was driving, and sometimes it's hard to tell them two apart. They've been friends their whole life. Cam is family, and we never had to question his loyalty. He always said he was our ride or die, now he just took one for the team.

Tank finally called me, and I almost dropped my phone when I saw his name pop up.

"Tank! What the fuck, where are you!" I shouted. "I'm at Crossway, get here asap" he said in a low tone. Crossway was a safe house only a few of us knew about which is probably why he called me first. We just bought the property a month ago. It wasn't much furniture in it yet only a bedroom set for one of the rooms. My mom and grandmother didn't even know about that one, they only knew about our first safe house on the south side. I decided to switch locations because too many knew about the first one, we just hadn't announced it yet. I wasn't even sure if Tank told Blue.

"Me and Blue are going to go get Tank." I told my mom & Nana and said they should go back to the party, we'll figure everything out and come back before the party ends. We drove off.

"B you familiar with Crossway?" I asked to see if he knew about it yet. "Are you talking about the spot you and Tank just copped? Yeah I been there once" I was relieved he knew. I told Blue to get in my car with me, I needed to be the one driving.

I didn't want to call Will while Blue was in the car. I wasn't sure if he knew that was our real father or not, but I had a feeling Will had nothing to do with this. We didn't talk all the time, he would only take me to dinner about once a month.

After what he said when we first met, I figured I'd keep him close. Tank still didn't want anything to do with him, and Will was pretty upset about that. He seemed like a nice guy, but like I mentioned, I was only keeping in contact with him for my own reasons. I needed somebody close to the law in my corner or at least on call. I didn't trust him at all, but I could tell he would do whatever I wanted him to do.

We pulled up to Crossway and I told Blue to go in and get Tank. I didn't even see if Tank knew what happened over the phone, but news travels fast so I'm sure he knew by now. And if he did, I knew he was a total wreck. Blue went to the backdoor and Tank was there waiting on him.

"I'll be right back" I yelled out. I was going to drive around for a couple blocks and call Will. I didn't want Tank to know I'd been talking to him. We had a big argument the last time we talked about Will and Tank had me fucked up because he was tryna say I was police too. The way we been moving, we needed somebody on the other side, and that's something he couldn't seem to understand.

"Officer Will speaking" he answered. I called him from my other phone, a number he wouldn't recognize.

"Will its Tia, please tell me you know what's going on" I asked him. I didn't want him to know that his name was mixed in it yet.

"I'll text you an address to meet me at in an hour. Sorry about your brother" Then he hung up. *"My brother"* I thought to myself. Since its clear that Tank wasn't the one who was shot, why would he be so certain. Tank was his son too but he ain't sound too pressed or concerned. Fuck him!

Couple of weeks passed by since the accident. Cam survived, but he was still hospitalized and in critical condition. It was hard on all of us, I was calling and checking on him and his family every day. To survive 10 bullets was a major blessing and we made sure him or his family didn't want for anything.

We moved Cam to a private hospital the day of the accident at a private location about an hour away from where we lived that had 24-hour surveillance throughout the whole building. Nobody would be able to find him, not even the police. We paid off everybody to keep their mouths closed, the receptionist, other hospital staff, all the way up the doctors. They didn't give a fuck about him anyway, another black man shot up was the norm in this city. I needed everybody to deny Cam even being there. We even paid off his hospital bills in advance. I even had to go up to the news station and pay them to not run the story. We all dipped in our savings coming out of about $80,000 for everything.

Tank was still taking everything pretty hard. We haven't been working like we usually do because of the accident and not knowing who to trust. I needed to think of something to get us back to our grind. A new business, new hustle or something, but we needed to lay low. Seem like all our spots were being watched so we had to double up on security. This accident was a big lost, but I knew me and my team would bounce back as soon as it all was over.

One of my get money girls, Meya, was dating Cam, even though I didn't want nobody in our circle dating, I figured it'd be best so we wouldn't have to worry about any outsiders. She was by his side every day and every hour, so she wasn't trying to work at all. Even if she was physically ready to get back to work, mentally she was still a wreck. We all know in this game you gotta have your head on straight no matter what. Meya told me that her and Cam had been doing a little contest together to see who could stack the most money in 90 days. They were straight grinding and not spending any unnecessary money. She assured to me that she was straight and could afford to miss work to take care of Cam. Meya has always been the realest one on my team.

I never met with Will the day of the accident, what he said didn't sit well with me. I blocked his number from my phone, I didn't even want to see his name or hear his voice until I had everything figured out.

Everything seemed to be crashing down and it was up to me to remain focused and not let this situation bring me and my family down. Nobody on the streets knew anything about the hit, all they ever said was they heard a cop set it up. Nobody else said Wills name though, I was waiting for it. Even though I was already down 40k for Cam, I was still willing to put whatever on the persons head who shot him.

One day I randomly decided to unblock Will and see exactly what he had to say. If the streets didn't know any details, then I had to get to the bottom of it somehow. I texted him an address to meet me at in 2 hours. That's all the time he had to clear his name because if he didn't show up, he was just as guilty as whoever set it up.

I arrived at the location about 30 minutes early and ordered me a glass of wine. When he came in, he didn't have his police get up on, that was the first red flag. He usually works the day shift that's how I was certain he would be able to meet me. I gave him a dry greeting as he proceeded to sit down. I was a little buzzed at the time, but still on my square.

"Tia a lot has happened since the last time we talked, I've been trying to reach out to you and…." "Save it Will" I cut him off. I didn't have time to hear no sob stories or nothing like that. I needed to know who shot at my family and why everybody was so certain a cop was behind it. I looked at him with a serious face.

"Did you have anything to do with my brother being shot?" I stared at him and waited for a reply. I said my brother on purpose to make him think Tank was the one shot, since the hit was for him anyway.

"Tia, I promise you I had nothing to do with what happened. Is Tank okay?" he asked as his eyes started to get glossy. I guess paying off the hospital staff worked, since he didn't know it was Cam that was shot, I decided to play along.

"My brother is dead and whoever killed him is just as dead" I said in a serious tone. The way Will was looking I just knew he was about to break down and embarrass me in this bar. So, I added fuel to the flame. "We had a private funeral and buried him next to his father." Now I usually don't play about death like this, but I needed to do whatever I had to do to get to the bottom of what happened. Will stood up and I looked at him confused. I think he could tell that I was lying or something.

He looked at me right in my eyes and said, "If Tank was dead you wouldn't be able to sit here and say it so calm" I was impressed. I forgot we did have a spiritual connection. He kept going, "I'm not sure what happened to Tank but something is telling me he's not dead. I will tell you anything you want but please don't lie to me about anything like that" I grew irritated.

"Nigga tell me who the fuck shot up my brothers' car." I was pissed because he wasn't in the position to make any demands.

"Calm down Tia" he said in a low tone. "Do you know about the relationship between Tasha and my old partner Hobbs?" he asked me. Tasha was Cam's mother, I was confused.

"No" I replied dryly. He continued, "Well from my understanding they had something to do with the hit. Once I heard that I quit the force, I couldn't continue to have coworkers that were dirty like that, especially not ones who were attacking my distant family.

"So, what does Tasha have to do with anything?" I asked him. I was trying to hold my composure but all I could think about was how she came in the hospital screaming that day.

Will went on and told me that Hobbs and Tasha broke up about a couple months ago. She was one of his informants and would get information from her son about you guys and go back to Hobbs. When they broke up Hobbs was furious because she no longer contacted him, he knew he couldn't do anything legal because they had a romantic relationship. A couple of days after they broke up, Hobbs found out that all the things she told him were lies. She played him and he's been looking for revenge.

I couldn't even take in everything that was being said, my first thoughts were Big A in my head telling me not to trust anybody. This story sounds fishy but Tasha was lowkey a crackhead so I wouldn't be surprised at anything she did, but why. Why would she agree to rat if she was only going to give the wrong information? Only answer I could think of was that she wanted to protect Cam.

Will told me that he confronted Hobbs in private and Hobbs denied having anything to do with the hit. Then the next thing Will told me had to ready to catch a case right then and there. "Hobbs been working with the Black crew, they got him in their pockets." The black crew has been our enemies ever since Big A was alive, he tried to squash the beef but once he died it all started over again. Tank and Cam were moving big weight and those Black crew niggas were jealous of them, they were jealous of all us. I wouldn't be surprised if they tried to put the hit out for Tank. So that got me thinking, Tasha must of knew about the black crew and was using Hobbs to protect Cam. I would have to talk to her about that, not sure why she thought nobody would find out.

I apologized to Will for lying earlier and told him that Cam was the one shot. I didn't tell him anything about our locations, but I assured to him that Tank was in one piece.

We were about to part ways and when I stood up, I decided to give Will a hug and my big hoop earrings got caught on his sweater. He removed his sweater without even thinking and guess what I saw, a fucking wire. I could tell he tried to disguise it but being in the game I knew exactly what a wire looked like. This man just played me, I acted like I didn't see it and just continued to walk towards the door.

I knew that story sounded like some bullshit. When I got in my car, I started to fell so much anger and rage, then I made a phone call with my other phone and once I ended the call, I felt relieved. I never thought in a million years I would have to arrange in the murder of my real father, but he was just as guilty as Hobbs. I stopped at home and grabbed $15,000 out of my safe and they would get the other 10 after the job was done. I knew it would be a hard because Will is police, but I didn't care. I wanted him dead by the end of the week.

TO BE CONTINUED......

# WORSE NEW YEARS EVER

CYNIQUA MAREE

Here it was New Year's Eve and my man was nowhere to be found. I had been blowing up his phone since 6pm, and now it's almost 10 o'clock and he still hasn't returned my call.

"I know this man better not be out with another bitch." I thought to myself. Seem like the same things keep happening over and over. Crazy thing is, we've been doing good ever since he proposed to me in front of all our family and friends on Thanksgiving. That was happiest day of my life. I should have known he was up to something because he wanted Thanksgiving dinner at our house and told me to invite everybody. I felt like the luckiest girl in the world.

Now my man wasn't perfect, he had cheated before, and had me in some pretty harsh situations but I forgave him each time. No matter what I know that he loves me, and I love him too.

So here I am looking fine as wine, my mink brazilian hair was curled to perfection and I had on a black all-purpose one piece. Meaning that I could either throw on some tennis shoes or heels and it would still look fire. The one piece fit so perfect on my curves I just knew my man would be drooling all over me ready to take it off.

I paced the floor and thought to myself "He better not be at his baby mothers house" That girl been bugging ever since we got engaged. I know she wish it was her with the 5-carat engagement ring, pushing the 2019 Range Rover, living in the 3-bedroom condo downtown Chicago like we were. I ain't no hater though, baby mother wasn't doing too bad for herself. She lives in a nice single-family house in the suburbs that my man put her in way before he met me, but she still holds her own. and she drives a 2015 BMW that he paid cash for so her and his 2 kids can get around.

That's why I love Trey so much because no matter what he's always had a big heart and he's never been selfish. His heart and personality definitely matched his looks too. Trey was one of those men who been fine their whole life. 6'5, caramel brown skin, with a pearly white smile. I love that he has a big heart, but of course I didn't too much care for him paying majority of baby mothers bills, but he always explains it as he's paying his kids bills and not hers, so I guess it was okay.

One thing he didn't play about were his children. I couldn't wait to have his baby one day; his kids were beautiful so I just know our babies would be gorgeous. Now Trey always had a lot of money, but he wasn't no drug dealer or anything like that, he's always been a hustler since a teenager and that's how he got in the position he's in now. He owned a car dealership and invested in different properties. Just like every other successful person around here. We all knew that real estate was the real way to get rich. Unlike a lot of people, he didn't allow his self to be blinded by material things, and that's the main reason his bag was super secured.

During the 3 years me and Trey been together, it's been plenty of times where I had to pop up at his baby mothers house just to make sure he wasn't over there sneaking and geeking, blowing her back out like he was doing mine. It was this one night I actually did catch him over there. A couple of busted windows and slashed tires let them know I wasn't the one to play with, since they didn't want to open the door. His baby mother didn't want no smoke, she was scared of me. Which is why I never understood why she would try to seduce him. I know for a fact he wasn't checking for her, but she knew one mention of his kids, he was there asap.

After a while it slowed down, but now I'm guessing it never stopped. If Trey really thought I was going to marry him with these same back and forth games going on he had another thing coming. Good thing I had Michelle's *(his baby mother)* number on speed dial. I never hesitated to call her when I needed to. Plus, I used to keep her kids all the time so why wouldn't I have her number. It's not like Trey was there all the time with them. I didn't have a problem keeping them either, they were my babies and they loved me.

I gave Michelle a call. "Yes Keri" she answered like she had an attitude, like she forgot I'll black her eye again. "What's Up Michelle, did Trey stop by there?" She took a deep breath, it sounded like she was moving around or something.

"No Keri he didn't, and I been calling his ass all day, he was supposed to take the kids to his mama while I get ready to go out." I was not trying to listen to this girl whine, but I let her continue.

"He always pulling shit like this now I gotta drive all the way to the north side then come right back this way. Where you at? You think you can take the ki...." CLICK!! I hung up right in her face, I don't have time for no favors bitch I'm looking for my man just like you are looking for him.

Now if he ain't with Michelle, where is he at?? I thought to myself. I wasn't even going to let Trey ruin my night, he's does that plenty of times already. It was New Year's Eve I was about to go outside. I talked to my girls earlier so I already had a plan B. Good thing I had another apartment in Gary close to my friends so I would be able to get fucked up and not have to drive all the way back downtown. So from this point on it was fuck Trey, he'll be sleeping alone tonight. I called him one more time and now his phone is going straight to voicemail. I didn't know what to think, so I didn't think at all, I got him off my mind.

I called up my girls and let them know I was on the way. I stopped at the liquor store and grabbed a half gallon of anejo patron, I was about to enjoy my night and bring in the new year lit, with or without Trey.

I got to my girl Missy crib and she was still getting dressed. I didn't know exactly where we were going but it definitely wasn't going to be a club. We just weren't in that kind of mood this year. We were all at Missy's crib drinking, dancing, singing all the way up until midnight. Still no word from Trey. Any other time I would have been worried, but the patron in me said forget about him.

My girl Sasha got a phone call about a hotel party not too far from where we were at, so we hopped in my range rover and headed to see what it was looking like. We pulled up at the Hilton and it seemed to be a lot of cars outside. I'm not the smartest person in the world, but it ain't too many people I know driving an all-black Tesla around here. Once I took a peep at the license plate, I was for certain that was Treys car. I've never knew him to be associated with the homies whose hotel party it was, so why is my man at the Hilton on New Year's Eve and not with his fiancé?

I was trying my best to play it cool and keep quiet at first, but Sasha yelled out, "Kerri, ain't that Treys car over there?" I tried to act like I didn't see it for real. "Where? All these cars look the same" I said in a low tone. "Bitch stop playing who else you know pushing an all-black Tesla round here?" She said while giving me a funny look. "Well let's go in this party and see if he in here" I said back to her.

Nobody else spoke we all just fixed our hair and makeup and proceeded to get out of the car. I'm glad I had already been drinking because my hands were shaking badly. I didn't know what to expect. I wasn't going to cause a scene though, I was going to walk up to him calmly and tell him to step outside. Then I was going to cause a scene, he really had me fucked up.

We all walked in the room where the party was at, I mentally scanned the room so fast I didn't even here or see one of my good friends Boose walk up to me.

"K, you fucked up that bad you can't hear a nigga" Boose said loudly knocking me out of my trance. My first thought was to blow him off but once I finally took a look at him and saw how fine he was looking. I lost my train of thought. He had on a Gucci button up shirt and Gucci loafers, fresh lining with his beard looking perfect. My eyes got wide and I almost forgot all about Trey for a second.

It's been a while since I saw Boose, so we definitely had some catching up to do. I didn't see Trey in the suite though, so I had Sasha walk back outside with me only to see that his car was gone. It's like he must of knew I was there or something. I called his phone a couple more times, it was still going straight to voicemail. At this point I could tell he had me on the blocklist. We hopped in my truck, rolled a blunt and took a couple more shots of that patron, then went back into the party.

Now this time as I walk into the party my attention was focused on Boose, so I went and sat next to him. We talked, joked, and laughed the whole night. We were in the party for a couple more hours and everybody was just about fucked up, especially Missy. She was the one who claimed she wasn't going to drink like that so she would drive, but she looked more drunk then me. Of course Sasha wasn't going to drive because she didn't have a license and was always scared of getting pulled over. Boose offered to drive my truck and take all of us home. He said he'll have his brother pick him up after.

Boose dropped everybody off which I can't really remember because I dozed off in the front seat, but when I woke up, we were outside of my apartment.

"How did you know I was coming here" I asked him. "I didn't, but I figured you wasn't going back downtown in those conditions." He said. He was right. Boose was always like a brother I never had, but I never called him my brother or anything because I knew he always had a crush on me. We've been there for each other on plenty occasions just based off the fact we've been friends so long. I never acted funny towards him when I got with Trey, but we didn't talk to each other all the time like we used to.

Soon as I stepped into my apartment I walked straight to my bedroom and flopped down on my bed. I wasn't even worried about if Boose had a ride back to his car or not, he knew he could crash here if he wanted. I was so drunk the only thing I took off were my shoes. Boose came to my door and yelled "You good K?" I just shook my head yeah.

"Come in here B, you can turn on the tv if you want" He walked in and sat on the edge of the bed. We made eye contact and if my eyes could talk, I know they were telling him I wanted him. I laid back and Boose started slowly creeping up to me and my only thoughts were, whatever happens, happens. I wasn't about to tell him no either.

He pulled the sleeves down off my shoulders and next thing I knew I was laying there with only my black lace thong on and bra that

50

matched. He slipped my thong down and started going to work with his thick tongue.

Me and B had never been intimate before so I really didn't know what to expect, but the way that his tongue was swirling all over my clit in perfect motions and a perfect rhythm, I could tell he'd been wanting to do this for a long time. I couldn't even talk. He kept going nice and gentle. It was the best head I ever had in my 28 years of living. He was way better then Trey.

"Oh my God baby, I'm about to cum" I screamed out. That's when he sped it up and I couldn't do nothing but cum all over his face. I felt like he took my soul and he licked it all up not leaving a trace.

"Damn B" was all I could say. He stood there for a minute licking his lips and unbuckling his pants. In my mind I was thinking, "What if this changes things? What if it ruins our friendship? I'm engaged, I know Trey has been doing me wrong, but 2 wrongs don't make a right." I guess Boose could sense my uncertainty, so he whispered, "If you don't want to, I'll understand. I'm not pressuring you into anything"

Now why did he say that? That just made me want him more. "I'm okay B, you think I was gonna just let you leave that easy" I pulled him by his arm, and he flopped on the bed. I finished taking his pants off and his dick was so big. I was so drunk, and I didn't give a damn, I was about to suck the skin off of it. I put his manhood deep into my mouth and all I could hear were the moans that he was making. That only made me go harder and made my pussy o wet. I loved to suck dick when I was drunk because I never gagged, it made me feel like a pro. Just as he was about to cum, I stopped and let him cool down for a minute. Then I slid on top of his dick and it felt so good. I tilted my head back and started riding him slow, then fast, then slow again. I didn't let him do anything I wanted him to cum while I was on top of him and by the way I was stroking my body up down, I'm sure he knew that too.

We both came together and when I slid off of him, I started to feel bad. I wonder what's next, I wasn't about to let that good head dick just fade away, I needed that on the regular. I didn't say anything to him I just went to the bathroom to take a shower. By the time I got out of the shower, B was gone.

"Damn" thinking to myself, did I just get finessed? Even if I did, I liked it and wouldn't mind doing it again. I tried calling Trey again, still no luck. So I took my last shot of patron and just prayed to God that nothing bad happened to my fiancé.

I woke up the next morning with a banging headache trying to pull myself out of bed, but I just couldn't do it. I looked around my room and wondered why I was even at this apartment when I never came here. I searched the bed to find my phone and once I grabbed it, it was dead. First thing came to my mind was Trey and suddenly all of last night's events came back to me. I really can't believe he brought in the new year without me.

A dark feeling come over my body as I charged my phone waiting for it to power on. "I really hope nothing bad happened to Trey" I thought to myself. Even though he's cheated on me in the past, he's never pulled a disappearing act. When I used to find out he was cheating on me with other women, it was rarely because of something he did. It was all of those "I'm coming to you as a woman" ass bitches. They knew about me and knew they couldn't compare to the type of woman I was, so their only option was to be messy. It was always weird to me because I talked to my man all the time, when does he ever have a chance to cheat? Anyway, I got right down on my knees prayed to God that nothing bad has happed to Trey. My phone finally powered on and Sasha must have knew that because her call came straight through.

"Hello" I answered in a dry voice. "Bitch get up, I think I left my purse in your truck last night and I need it, can you check for me please" she asked. "Sasha, fuck a purse right now why were we so fucked up last night" I said in a playful tone while I got up to look for my keys. I couldn't find them. They weren't in my purse, wasn't laying around, they were really gone.

"Let me call you right back boo I can't find my keys" I said to her and didn't even give her a chance to respond before I hung up the phone. I searched high and low for my keys and then something told me to look out the window, and I saw that my truck was gone.

"What the fuck Boose" was all I could say. Why would he take my truck without telling me? This isn't even like him, he was always polite and respectful when it came to me. Now I see why he left when I was in the shower.

I called his phone and it went straight to voicemail. Is this really how 2020 was starting off? I even tried to call Trey again, same thing. It's some weird shit going on, and I'm about to get to the bottom of it.

I called Sasha back she answered on the first ring. "Did you find it?" she asked. "I need you to come to my low spot right now, it's an emergency" I told her and I'm sure she could hear the anger in my voice.

Sasha got to my crib in less than 15 minutes. She texted me when she was outside, and I told her to come up. "Where is your truck boo?" she asked me, looking confused. "That nigga Boose took my shit, and now he ain't answering" I told her. I really couldn't believe what was happening. He knew I would let him use my truck if he really needed to be somewhere but taking it behind my back was really foul.

"You talked to Trey yet?" Sasha asked me, but I just shook my head no. I called my big brother Kevin, he was always the first person I would call whenever I had a situation going on.

"Good morning sis, Happy New Year" he said to me in a sleepy voice. "Bro I need you asap, where you at?" I knew he could tell something serious was going on because I heard him starting to make noise in the background like he was putting on clothes.

"I'll be there in 5 minutes, don't say shit over this phone" My brother was a big drug dealer in Gary and he always talked about not saying shit on over the phone. He caught a couple cases throughout the years so whenever it was something going on, he'd rather talk in person. My brother got there on exactly 7 minutes. I told him everything about what happened the night before, from Trey not answering to me having sex with Boose and now my truck being missing. "Did you track it sis" he said. I felt slow because why I didn't think of that. My Range Rover had GPS tracking on it and I had the app on my phone to see exactly where it was at.

Once a location popped up to where my truck was at, we headed out. When we pulled up, we were at an old abandoned church and I didn't my truck anywhere. "Stupid ass iPhone" I said out loud. Kevin stepped out of the car to make a few phone calls, he knew Boose but never really fucked with him like that. I was so angry because I felt like my life was doing a whole 360 when everything was just starting to come together. I tried calling Trey and Boose again, no luck. My brother slowly walked back to the car and I could tell whatever was said on that phone call wasn't good.

"Sis, you're not going to like what I'm about to say. Before I tell you what I just found out I need to be upfront about some things." My heart fell to the ground because I knew this wasn't about to be good.

"Trey is my boy, he's like another brother to me, but it's a lot that you don't know about him. We had a talk some weeks ago and he assured to me that he would come clean about everything he had dealings with" he said slowly.

"What the nigga got another bitch or something?" I shot back, eager for him to just say what he gotta say. "No, your man is in the game and he's deep in the game too sis" he told. I couldn't really process what he was trying to say.

"The drug game?" I asked him.
"Yes, and right now he's in trouble"
"What kind of trouble"
"All I can say is, how much yall got saved up because yall going to need it.
"I'm not understanding bro, please just be straight forward."

The more he began to talk, to the more I felt weak to my knees. Trey wasn't out last night cheating on me, some bum ass niggas kidnapped my man and now they want ransom money. This isn't the Trey I knew, I thought everything he did was legit, how could he let this happen. I didn't know what to think or say.

"One more thing sis" Kevin said as he was trying to calm me down in the backseat. This was the worse day of my life. "How much do I need?" I asked him in between sobs. "They want $75,000 by tomorrow or they're going to kill him." I could tell he as hurt too just by the way he said those words to me. I kept calling Trey's phone and it was still going to voicemail. I tried calling Boose again and surprisingly he picked up.

"Boose what the fuck, where are you with my shit" I screamed. Boose stayed quiet for a few seconds and he said. "If you want to see this truck or see your man again. Have my 75k ready by tomorrow morning" then he hung up. I burst into tears. I can't believe I just slept with the enemy.


TO BE CONTINUED.....

# RIGHT PLACE, WRONG TIME

CYNIQUA MAREE

I was shocked to see it was pouring down raining once again in Detroit, but other than that it was a normal Wednesday for me. I was looking good, feeling good, and my money was even better. I looked down at my phone to see it was almost 7pm. I was almost done hustling for the day.

Shortly after I found myself at Smooths Sports Bar & Grill, not too far from my stomping grounds. Me and my homies would kick it up there to eat and have drinks almost every Wednesday. It was something about Smooths that everybody loved, because even though it was pouring cats and dogs outside, it was still a nice sized crowd inside.

We walked in and headed to our normal table right in front of the flat screen to watch the game. I scanned the place when I first walked in, and saw this gorgeous queen sitting at the bar. I had never saw here in there before. She was caramel brown skinned with her natural curly hair flowing across her shoulders. She had on a navy-blue Milano jogging suit and from the way she was sitting down I could tell she was super thick. I tried not to stare at her or be thirsty, but I couldn't keep my eyes off of her. I could tell she wasn't from around here.

I told one of my partners I was going to holla at her even though we all had been giving her the eye. I never had a problem when it came to the ladies, so my confidence was always sky high.

Once I started walking closer to her it looked like she was making a funny face towards me then she started turning up her nose. "Yeah this chick definitely doesn't know who I am?" I thought to myself, but in a weird way it kinda turned me on. I was so used to women throwing themselves at my me because of my name and my money but talking to a chick that didn't know anything about me was probably what I needed.

"How you doing gorgeous, what you drinking?" I said as I walked close to her, but she didn't reply. She just looked at me then back into her phone like I wasn't even there. I noticed she had a unique aura to her, soon as I was drawn into her, she hadn't even spoke yet. My first thoughts were, "I had to have her."

Before I walked over to her I figured she was waiting on somebody because she had been sitting there by herself and kept looking towards the entrance. When she ignored me, I didn't get the feeling she wanted me to leave her alone, so I repeated myself and made sure I spoke a little louder. She was fine but I didn't take being ignored too lightly. Once I see something I want, I gotta have it no matter what. The second time I spoke she replied. "Oh, I'm sorry love, I'll have a strawberry long island" she said as she started to look me up and down. I called the bartender over, which just so happens to be my cousin Dede.

Dede was my first cousin and we've been close since we were kids. Her husband is the owner of Smooths, but he basically let her run it. She has a bachelor's degree in accounting and has been bartending on the side for years. Everything that went on in that bar, she knew about it. She even lets me and my homies clean money through there from time to time. Dede used to do fraud for years until she married Smooth, but they'll still be times when she would dip and dap if it was worth it. She was a pro at that shit but was slowly transitioning to the legit life. I was proud of her, that girl had long money.

After Dede took our order and came back with the drinks, she handed them to us, and I saw she had a small smirk on her face. She then turned to shorty like she was throwing shade or something. It was a bit weird because Dede always helped me bag the ladies that would come through there. I took a mental note to get back with her later on that and focused my attention to this beauty that was in front of me.

"That's my cousin Dede she's the owner, I'm Mack and what's your name?" I said in a soft tone but loud enough for her to hear me.

"My name is Lynn" she said.

We started to talk a little more and after about 10 minutes I realized we both had a lot in common. Even though she was communicating with me she was giving me the type of vibe like she wasn't too interested. I started to feel salty because once again this was something that I wasn't used to.

I was the big dawg around here and most of the time the women would approach me, especially since I've been known as a bachelor. I've been having my way with the ladies since I was a youngin' and even though I was getting older, I wasn't ready to settle down with nobody. Shorty was throwing me off, but actually turning me on at the same time. I learned a lot about her within that short amount of time, and I could tell I would have to have a different approach when it came to her.

My phone started ringing and when I saw the number, I knew it was time for me and the brothers to head out and make couple more moves before we headed home. I didn't even ask Lynn for her number, I was just hoping I would run into her again.

I know most niggas try to act like they be out here putting in work, but we were really about that action. We had about 4 trap houses around our city, plenty workers from teenagers still in high school to old heads we knew from around the way. This foundation we got right now started from the mud and its rock solid. I be so busy getting to the money I don't really have time for relationships and dating. Women these days always want something right after we fuck, rather its some money a bag, shoes. I don't mind tricking on the ladies though. Those type of women I don't take too seriously, I just play my role.

I got one daughter and she live in Atlanta with her mother and some corn ball ass nigga that married my baby mama. I was mad at first that she took my daughter away from me, but eventually I got over it.

I started visiting Atlanta more often and began doing business there. It was a decent city, but I couldn't see myself moving there. I invested in my baby mama beauty salon and now she was about to open up her own kids' boutique. I knew she was doing well for herself when she sent me $5,000 for my birthday. I didn't want to accept it but she assured to me that I deserved it for investing in her. One thing about my baby mama is that she always been a real bitch, I still loved her, but I loved the streets more. Her husband was cool too, we would make money moves together when I would come to Atlanta to visit. That was like black Hollywood, you could make money anywhere out there. As long as my daughter was well taken care of I had no reason to trip. I even thought about buying a house out there and maybe one day giving to my daughter when she turned 18. I just knew I wasn't about to leave Detroit though, I had too many seeds that I've planted throughout the years and I needed to be close to them while they grow. My baby mama was even teaching my daughter how to be an entrepreneur at only 6 years old, so I knew 10 years from now she would be ahead of the game.

The following week, me and my homies were at Smooths at little earlier than we'd usually be to grab some food before a big drop. I really wasn't trying to be kicking it while we had business to handle, but we hadn't ate shit all that day, and these niggas acted like they were about to die. It usually wasn't that packed at Smooths this early in the day, so I figured we'd be good with a couple of hours to spare. This really not how we did business and I made a mental note to have a talk with them later after the drop.

We walked into the bar and had Dede take our orders. Ever since I woke up that day, I'd been having a funny feeling, like the whole day was just off. I ignored that feeling though because it was a lot of money to made and I couldn't get distracted. I ain't the type of dude to be nervous and all that either. Once Dede gave me my shot of Hennessy, I threw it back and shook that feeling off. We ain't have that much time to kick it so I didn't get too comfortable, I kept my eyes on the clock and on my phone. The homies were talking bullshit about what they were gonna wear for All Star weekend in Chicago, but I stayed focused. I don't even think I was going to make that drive. It was about to be a lot going on during that weekend and I really didn't have time for it.

I glanced up at the front door and to my surprise shorty from the other day walked in with one of her friends. She was looking fine as hell, even better than when I saw her the first time. Once again, I couldn't keep my eyes off of her, I must have been staring into space because I hadn't even noticed Dede walking back over to our table.

"Aye cuz, that's a bad bitch I can't even deny it, but I got a funny feeling about her, something just ain't right" Dede said to me. I wasn't trying to hear nothing she was talking about at the time, I needed to see what was up with Lynn. Sometimes Dede didn't know when to mind her business, but I did appreciate her for looking out. I just nodded and replied okay. Then I told Dede to send Lynn and her friend 2 strawberry long islands, and whatever else they wanted on me.

We still had about an hour and half until our drop, so I figured I had a little time to spare to shoot my shot at Lynn again. I walked over to her and proceeded to shoot my shot again. Soon as I got close to her, she started being really nice to me. It caught me off guard, because I was prepared for a challenge like she gave me the other day. I don't know if she was acting different because her girl was with her or what. I was feeling the vibe though. The first time I saw her, she a bit dressed down with the jogging suit, but this second time shorty was looking sexy as fuck. I wanted her so bad, the way her friend was looking I wanted her too.

I was the man around town, so Lynn probably went and did her homework. I guess she realized she was in the presence of a real street nigga. I actually wanted to date her, I don't care where she wanted to go, I would take her and show her how a solid nigga from the D get down. We started off with a little small talk, I could tell that she was getting tipsy from the drinks I bought her. Seems like that stuck up attitude she had when I first met her went right out the window. She was laughing and giggling at every little thing I was saying, then she started touching all on me and giving me this look like she wanted to fuck. My first instinct was to dip off in the bathroom with her, but I didn't say anything. I just continued to read body language and paid close attention to the things she was saying. I really ain't want this opportunity to pass me by so I was thinking I had to make a move quick.

"I'll be right back baby, don't go nowhere" I told her as I walked over to the table my homies were at. I told them what I was on, and that I'd be right back. We rode to the bar in 3 separate cars and even though I didn't want to ride with all this money and product in my car, their cars had way more, so I was willing to take the risk.

My guys were smart, and we were successful, so we moved different then a lot of other niggas out here, so I know they'd be cool. We had a whole hour left until it was time to leave so I was about to take Lynn to the closest hotel and give her what she been asking for.

Before we left, I made sure her friend was good and gave her money to order anything else she wanted. Lynn was the one that drove them, so she left her friend the keys to her car in case she needed to leave before we came back. I paid for everybody's tab then we walked out and headed to my car. In the back of my mind I was thinking why did Lynn all of a sudden go from 0-100. As soon as we got in the car shorty started kissing all over me, unbuckling my pants, moaning and just wilding. She was acting like this was something she wanted to do her whole life, and I was loving every minute of it. I started driving and next thing I know she pulled up her skirt and started playing with her pussy right in front of me. My dick was so hard, and her pussy was so pretty.

"I want you right now daddy, I can't wait" she said as she stuck 2 fingers in her pussy then into her mouth. After that she pulled out my manhood and started giving me some of the best head I ever had in my life.

"Damn baby, you gonna make me crash" I said in between moans. She deep throated me, sucked me, licked on my balls, all types of shit. Shorty was going so crazy I could barely focus on my surroundings.

She lifted her head up and said, "Let's go to the hotel right on 183rd" and the way she was making me feel, I would just about agree to anything she wanted me to. That wasn't the hotel I had in mind though. The way that girl tongue was moving I couldn't drive the way I wanted, and I'm sure I was swerving more than a little bit. I stopped at a red light and she was still going, wouldn't even lift her head up when I asked her to.

I checked my surroundings and I saw a black SUV approaching behind me at the light and as I was making a left turn, I noticed the truck looked like 12. I didn't even get more than 2 blocks before they flashed their lights at my car. "FUCK" I said out loud then Lynn lifted her head up to see what was wrong. When she saw the red and blue lights, she hurried to put her clothes back on and I did the same thing. My heart dropped to my ankles when I realized I still had that work in my car from earlier. I know one thing, they didn't need not one reason to try and search my shit.

"What do you want me to do?" she asked me while acting all nervous and weird. "Calm down baby, I got this" I told her, then I sent a group text out to all my people that said "611" and that would let them know, I may have got caught slipping once again. I shared my location with them too so I knew they would come flying to where I was, no questions asked.

I can't believe I let myself get in this situation all because of some hoe ass bitch. My dick was soft as fuck now. She looked over at me and could tell I was growing angry just by my facial expressions. I tried to hold it in so I could look good in front of these pigs.

"You need me to hide anything for you Reno? Guns, drugs, paperwork?" I quickly replied and said, "Nah shorty I got this, I ain't do shit anyway to get pulled over, at least I don't think I did." Then my eyes almost popped out my head as my thoughts took over.

"Why would this bitch ask if I had paperwork? And how the fuck shorty know my name when I gave her a fake name?" I told this lady my name was Mack and I know my cousin Dede didn't tell her because she wasn't fucking with her like that when she came to the bar. Now I was confused and began to stare at her so cold I could tell I was making her nervous. I didn't have time to ask her how she knew my real name because 2 officers started walking towards the car with their gun drawn.

"What the fuck" I said out loud. I raised my window down and they ain't ask for no license, insurance or nothing like it. He demanded I exit the car immediately. "Oh hell no, these muthafuckas not about to take another black man out" I said out loud. With my hands raised I asked, "Sir, can you tell me why I'm pulled over?" The police officer started getting loud and hostile with me, "Get your ass out the car now before I get you out myself" I slowly cut the car off and when I opened my door I noticed that these were federal agents pulling me over, not no regular police.

After he searched me, he told me to sit on the curb, and as I slowly made my way over there, I didn't see Lynn. I watched closely as they started searching my car and once they popped the trunk, I knew it was over for me. I held my head down and said a quick prayer. I didn't want to make any sudden movements because I know if I did, they would be quick to put a bullet in my head.

I continued to move slowly and what I saw next had me ready to lose my marbles and choke slam that bitch. Looks like she was working for 12 as an undercover this whole time. That kind of explains the weird shit she was saying in the car. My dumbass ran right into her fucking trap, I couldn't believe it. I knew I let my team down getting caught up like that so all I could do was hold my head down and prepare for everything that about to follow my mistakes. The federal agent came over by me and said, "You're good to go" with a pissed look on his face. I raised my head up, confused. I wasn't even driving the car with the secret compartment in it, so I knew all my product and some cash was back there. I stood up to look at my trunk and it was empty.

I turned around and saw shorty getting snapped on by who I could tell was her boss. A big smile came across my face as I got up and headed to the driver's seat of my car. Lynn was looking really shitty then all of a sudden, her beauty diminished in my eyes. I wanted to kill that hoe.

God was definitely on my side in this situation and I couldn't thank him enough, but I was still wondering what happened to all my shit that was actually supposed to be in the trunk. Soon as I got in the car, I picked up my phone to about 8 missed calls, but before I could unlock it Dede was calling so I drove off and accepted the call.

"Hey cousin, where you at you good?" she said yelling into the phone. I was still in shock from everything that just happened so quickly I couldn't even think straight. "Hello! You there?" she said even louder. I had to pull over into a McDonalds parking lot real quick. "Dede that bitch was a fed, how did I get fooled like that? I'm sick because I don't even play those pig games", I said to her in a calm tone. Dede didn't respond at first but then she took a deep breath and said, "Aye cuz you were tripping, and I could tell. Maybe you been going thru some personal shit, but I been trying to tell you this whole time that girl wasn't right. I just got a bad vibe from her from the day she walked into the spot." I couldn't even say nothing because she was 100% right. Then she proceeded to tell me about how she arranged for all my shit to get moved to the other cars once she noticed me and Lynn were getting touchy feely in the bar.

"Maybe the bitch put a spell on you or something, I've never saw you that googly over some pretty light skin bitch in the bar. Its plenty of bad bitches in Detroit and they all be at Smooths on the regular, I'm disappointed in you fam" She told me. Once again, I was lost for words, my favorite cousin just saved my life.

# BREAK UP
# LETTERS

CYNIQUA MAREE

Dear John,

By the time you find this letter I know that you'll already have an idea that I'm leaving you. The only reason I'm even writing this letter is so that you can reflect on the type of person you truly are, because for some reason you're in denial of your true self. I love you with all my heart, but I just can't deal with all the pain and abuse for any longer. After my last miscarriage I realized that none of our babies made it because that's not what God has in his plan. He didn't want me to have any attachments to you so now that I don't, it's getting easier for me to leave you.

The first time I was pregnant I was so happy to be carrying our first child, but it seems like you didn't share that same feeling. While I was going through my morning sickness, I was going through love sickness as well. You were never there for me, constantly cheating and just being an all-around bad person to me. I knew for a fact that once our child entered this world, you would be become a better man, but it's like I was holding on to false hope. I know you pushed me down the stairs so I could lose the baby. You claim it was an accident, but I could tell by the look in your eyes that's exactly what you wanted to happen. I thought you wanted our child, our family, but I guess you just had to take matters in your own hands. Little do you know; I know so much about you that you don't think. Your facial expressions describe your thoughts all the time. I never bring this to your attention, because I know that you would have tried to prevent it. It was just an evil look in your eyes, even when I cried and screamed for help you ignored me. Thank God I had my phone to call for help, if not you would have left me there to bear with the pain all by myself. When the ambulance arrived, you turned into a whole different person. The person I really wanted you to be, but as always you only act like that in front of other people.

    After I was discharged from the hospital, you beat me so bad when we got home it's like you didn't believe that the baby was gone, you had to make sure of it. I couldn't leave the house for weeks. I was going into deep depression from that tragic loss, and you just didn't give a fuck. I even thought about harming myself but luckily, I snapped out of it because I only wanted to die because you were in my life. You claim you love me so much, but the love you once showed me, faded away a long time ago. I'm tired of the cheating and disrespect, your dick is going to fall off and I should sue you for endangering my health. I've had multiple STDs and they all came from you. I heard the rumors of people saying you were on the down low. I defended you to the fullest, to the point where I fell off with one of my very best friends. Every time I think about it, I get sick to my stomach, then whenever I try to get you to be honest with me you beat on me. That told me the truth right there. I've already dealt with an abusive childhood and to think the man that claims he loves me treats me the same as my dysfunctional mother and father.

You think just because you have a lot of money you can be out here living foul, and that's something I'll no longer tolerate. Yeah, we have the big house and the nice cars, designer this and designer that, but it seems like the lifestyle was the only thing I was holding on to, because I stopped loving you a long time ago. I appreciate the things you did for me that helped me with my personal growth. You were the first man to ever invest in me the right way and since then my business has took off. The first few years we were together were some of the best times of my life. I really miss the old you, and once I realized that I would never have that person back, I decided to take matters into my own hands. We had so many good times, but it's like you turned into a monster, a person that I just did not know anymore.

I've been scared for my life, thinking that one day you would kill me and not just say it all the time. You've made me lose all my self-esteem, I wake up every day and just feel worthless. Good thing that I do have my hair company to run other than that I know depression would have taken over my life. You need serious help John, and I'm not sticking around to even see you get better. I want a man that loves me and shows me that he loves me. I want to wake up and instantly get butterflies, because I'm next to the man of my dreams. Sad to say, but you used to make me feel that way, not anymore.

The first time I caught you cheating was in our home, thank God you didn't have that bitch in our bed, but you tried to act like you were just friends with her, whole time yall were fucking. She was one of my clients, bought hair and wigs from me all the time. I didn't have an issue with her, because she doesn't owe me any loyalty. It's you, you were the one who should have at least been discreet. I don't know what I did to have you switch up on me like that. I had to go buy a gun just to feel protected in my own home. Not only did you invite your side bitch to where we laid our heads, but you invested in her the same way you invested in me. That's how I knew that there was no such thing as a main bitch, if it was, I sure wasn't it.

It's so many things that you've done throughout the years that has broken me, but I'd be sitting here writing all day and night. I am going to get all my thoughts off so that you can understand exactly why you won't see or hear from me again. My name is no longer Toyah, I've gotten a whole new identity, so you won't be able to track me down. I can finally have a real life with a real man. Yep, that's right, I've found somebody new and he's the one who had helped me build my confidence and build the strength to finally leave this hell hole I once called a home.

Do you remember when we went to your friends Superbowl party about a year ago? As soon as I walked into the house, I got a bad vibe and no longer wanted to be there. You threated to beat me up in front of everybody, so I just kept quiet and stayed to myself. Everyone could tell I was uncomfortable, but you didn't care. At the party, I went upstairs to use the bathroom and just burst out crying. I hated my life. Then your friend Ray knocked on the door to ask if I was okay. I was so lost in my thoughts I didn't realized that the bathroom door was unlocked. He walked in on me. Told me that if I made any loud noises, he would kill me right then and there. I was so confused because Ray was a sweetheart.

He walked over to me and told me how he's been wanting me since the first day he saw me. He put a knife to my throat and slowly undressed me, and as the tears flowed down my face the only thing, I could think of was why weren't you there to protect me. I couldn't believe that I was being raped while my man was just downstairs and didn't even notice I was missing for so long. Surprisingly Ray was not rough with me at all. I

83

was trying to break away, but he gripped my throat so tight, I almost passed out. He sucked and licked on my breast all the way down to my pussy. I was so scared I couldn't stop crying and just begged him to stop. He bent me over the bathroom sink and had his way with me until he was finished.

Somebody knocked on the door and I tried to cry out when I saw he didn't have the knife in his hand anymore. Its crazy because the person at the door was you. You called my name and then started to open the door. When you came in and saw what he was doing to me, you didn't even budge. I started screaming your name so loud and you just told me to shut the fuck up while closing the door behind you. After Ray was finish with me you came over and did the same thing. He didn't even have the decency to leave. He stayed and watched you fuck me just like he did. I thought it was a bad dream, so I just closed my eyes and waited for this nightmare to be over.

Next thing I know somebody else came to the bathroom and you threaten to kill me if I didn't let them have their way with me. That night I was raped by 3 of your friends and you didn't even care about how I felt. I wanted to leave you so bad that day but once again you said you would kill me if I did.

The next day you tried to explain that you "lost a bet" and instead of paying them the money you owed, you sold me like I was a piece of meat. That was the worse day of my life. I was such a clown because I still stayed with you. Before you walked out the house you left me $1,000 and told me I better not tell anyone. That's when I knew once again, you weren't the man for me anymore. That was the ultimate betrayal and I be damned if anything like that happened again. The crazy part is that I still love you, but I hate you at the same time. I hate myself for even allowing that abuse for so long. I can't wait to leave you and this house behind. I've saved up enough money to set up shop wherever I plan to move to. So, this is officially my last goodbye. All of my things are already out of the house and there is nothing you can do to stop me. I am so happy that I'm finally free. I was trying to make sure I was gone before you got here, but I think I just heard your car pull up in the driveway.

Dear Toyah,

Baby girl, you know that I'm the type of man that's going to always do and have whatever I want. Did you really think you was about to leave me that easily? You belong to me, I made you. It's my decision if I want you to leave or not, and it'll be a cold day in hell before I just let you walk out of my life. Anything I did to you, you deserved that shit. All you ever did was nag and complain every damn day. After a long of day of hustling and grinding, a nigga don't be wanting to hear that shit. How you gonna sit there and act like you was such a perfect woman, I know you only wanted me for my money. I didn't care though, I looked pass all of that. I couldn't even get a home cooked meal out of your ass. Once I got your business up and running you started feeling yourself. Yeah, I have other bitches, so what. That's what I want to do and nobody is gonna stand in my way. You act like you forgot who I was. I already had a bitch when I met you, but you were so blinded by the money you didn't a fuck, you just wanted your turn. I thought you would of got your turn and got out the way, but that was you who chose to stick around. I didn't make you do anything. That's your problem now you always worried about the wrong shit instead of worrying about how to please your man.

Bae girl that you caught in the house with me was really my friend, not matter what type of activities we engaged in, I could talk to her about anything and can't talk to you about shit. She even agreed to come into our bedroom with us, but you're such a boring bitch I didn't even bother to ask you.

One thing about you Toyah, you are an ungrateful woman. I gave you everything you wanted and needed and then some. Your wack ass parents used to treat you way worse than I did, and I don't see you writing letters to them and all that other shit. You must be a fool to think I was gonna let you get away from me that easily. Those teeth, that body and everything else belongs to me. I paid for that shit. You were shaped like a fat ass Mexican before you got with me, but just like any other gold-digging bitch, they get to feeling their self when they get their body done. You really got me fucked up, because who is this nigga you talking about you fucking with? I'll break your arm just like I did the first time. Ain't no nigga around here about to be smashing my bitch without my knowledge. Whoever the cornball ass nigga is, he gonna get what he got coming to him after you get what's coming to you.

So I see you wanna bring up the Superbowl party, but I knew you always had a thing for Ray I could tell. Every time the man would come over our house, you're being super nice all in his face like you wanted to fuck him, so I gave him green light. That's my pussy did you forget. I can give it away to whoever I want. You like that shit, and don't try to act like you didn't. I know about your past Toyah even though you thought it was a secret. I know how you used to be a hoe and had so many niggas paying for that pussy. You claim we gang raped you, but was that really your first time fucking multiple niggas in the same room? In the same day. Bitch I saved you. I never said I lost a bet to have them niggas fuck you, we wanted to have fun and your dry ass was ruining the energy, so I took matters in my own hands. If you didn't want Ray touching you, why you ain't scream for help? You waited until I walked in to act all sad and hopeless, but before that I know you liked that shit, that pussy was soaking wet by the time it was my turn. That's how I knew you were just a worthless hoe bitch. I hate that I had to do you like this because I love your ass, but this was the last and final straw.

Your letter was cute, I'm glad you got your thoughts off and I'm glad I got to the house when I did. I don't give a fuck about this house Toyah, I got 2 more cribs in the city that you don't even know about. I hated being in here with you that's why I was never home.

I could say I'm going to miss you Toyah, but actually I'm not. I'm going to always do what I have to do. You think you were just going to go and throw me under the bus. I don't know if you were going to the police or what. I can't have you destroying my life like you did yours. I have a baby boy on the way, and I have to do whatever to protect and take care of my family. I love you Toyah, but there was no way you were leaving this house alive, you asked for it. See you in hell when I get there.


Newscaster: Hi, this is Sharon Williams reporting live from Gary, Indiana where we have a rapid house fire that has killed at least one person. The victim's name is 32-year-old Toyah Rodriguez, she lived here in the home. Police got a call about a fire at approximately 6:09 pm. By the time fire fighters arrived, the victim had already been deceased. Police say this is not an accidental death, they believe the victim was killed right before the fire. So far, they have no leads on who could have caused this tragedy. If you have any information about this accident, please contact the local Gary police department. Back to you Trevor.

# STUCK IN THE GAME

I was in a deep sleep until I heard my phone ring and saw that it was my girl Normie facetiming me. "Wake up bitch it's time to go to work, I know you ain't still sleep" I looked at the clock and noticed it was already 6:30pm. "Oh shit". I couldn't be late to my makeup appointment, we were about to work at one of the biggest parties in Chicago tonight for one of the hottest rappers in the game. I can't believe I almost overslept and this all I been talking about for weeks.

It was Dice Birthday Bash, a big drug dealer turned rapper from out west and anything with his name on it was bound to be a sold-out event. Normie used to fuck with his older brother that's in the feds right now and Dice looked at us like family, we all grew up together. I already know the other strippers at the club was about to be on that hating jealous shit, because I already knew me and Normie was about to check a big bag tonight.

"I'm not drinking like that tonight G so I'm coming to pick you up and we can ride together" Normie told me before hanging up the phone. I jumped in the shower real quick, even though I took a shower earlier that day I needed to be freshly looking good, smelling good, the whole nine. We both got custom outfits made for the party and it was basically about to be a lit night.

She got to my house around 7:15 which was cool because our makeup appointments weren't until 8 & 8:30 so I told her to come in and pregame with me a little. I turned on the new city girls "You tried it" and started feeling myself.

"Oh, bitch look at this" Normie handed me her phone and showed me a text thread of this trick name Jack. We didn't know his real name and we didn't care to know as long as his money was real. He was a middle-aged Italian guy, and we would fuck with him from time to time. We did threesomes, stripper parties, sent pictures, videos, almost whatever he was willing to pay for. We've known Jack for years and genuinely loved him because he was easy to please, his money was long, and he always paid us top dollar. He's never been one of those weird tricks either, just a man that liked to have fun.

Jack was texting Normie telling her he wanted to see us tonight before he went out of the country for a month with his wife. I was thinking to myself why he would wait until the last minute to tell us. He knew we were always booked and busy.

"Damn, he really leaving for that long for real? We need to figure something out" I said in a serious tone while looking Normie directly in her eyes so she could feel my seriousness.

"What time you tryna get to work tonight?" she asked. I told her that we would just have to get there a little late. I'll text Dice to see what time they were planning on leaving out.

Actually, I'll facetime him, I'm sure he got a lot on to where he ain't responding to texts right now. I remember him telling us he had a radio interview at Power 92 before the party.

"The man Jack about to pay us extra" I said as I started to text him from Normies' phone. I told him we both wanted $2,500 a piece instead of the usual $1,500. He agreed just like I knew he would. He always made sure we were beyond satisfied. That had me thinking I should of asked for more, but its cool.

Jack has a suite at the W downtown that he pays monthly rent for, and that's where we always would meet. We agreed to be there by 10.

"I really hope Jack don't have us wasting too much time. You know Dice shooting a music video tonight too, and he's giving us $500 a piece for being in it, plus all the money they gonna throw on us." Normie said to me. She never told me how much they were paying, and once again I would of asked for more, but Dice was like family. Normie didn't really care for Jack as much as I did. I was dealing with him on my own for a while before I introduced them. It was the first time Jack wanted to have a threesome, and Normie was the first person I thought of being that we were already fucking with each other. A lot of people always thought me and Normie were in a relationship, but we were just best friends that liked to have fun.

We've been friends since high school and been through so much together. Anybody that knew us, knew we did not play about each other. I loved her so much and would do anything for her. The feeling was definitely mutual.

When I asked Normie to do the threesome with me and Jack, she was reluctant at first. Even though she danced at the club, she wasn't about that life outside of the club. I really wasn't either, but I was a vet in the game, and I had my own personal client list. It ain't like I would fuck with any nigga that came in the club and threw a bag. My list is mostly guys I used to date in the past, so why not fuck with them again and get paid while doing it? Jack was my homie and as long as his checks cleared, I made sure I kept him happy.

After our first threesome, Jack told me he really like Normie and wanted us to always see him together. She wasn't too hype about it at first, but I convinced her because at the end of the day, it was easy money. I even told Jack to contact her when he wanted to see us instead of me so she would get more into the habit of going on dates with him. Not only did he cash us out frequently, he was always knowledgeable. He would tell us about the stock trade, and always put us on to new ways to invest our money. He wanted to see us do good in life, he's always talked about the potential he sees in me. It's always good to have people like that around.

One thing about me I'm all about my money. I'm good at saving and I have a plan for my life that I had to stick to. So, it was always grind time for me. I didn't care about what people thought of me either, I'm a proud *paid* hoe. I ain't really been into exploiting myself though, I'm lowkey with my shit. Can't have everybody in my business, because I don't need nobody bringing up my past once I got rich and famous. Even if they did, I wouldn't care. Nothing or nobody can make me or break me.

When we got downtown to meet with Jack, we had valet take Normie's Audi. The suite was on the 14th floor, and when we knocked on the door Jack answered with a robe on and glass of champagne in his hand.

"Hello, my beautiful ladies, I've missed you both" he said as we both greeted him with a hug. Normie made a funny face on the slick side, then smiled to cover it up. I already knew she wanted to make this quick, I was on the same thing.

I took a glance at Jack and I could tell he had taken something. I knew right then and there we were really about to make this quick. I wasn't trying to mess up my makeup so I figured me & Normie would put on a show for him, collect our money and dip out. That's usually what we would do anyway. We only had about an hour to spare, little did he know.

It looked like Jack was trying to relax and chill, but I'm not surprised. Sometimes he just wanted us there to keep him company. I know Normie specifically told him we already had a prior engagement. I started to slowly take off my clothes in front of him then signaled Normie to follow my lead. Jack was looking a bit off. I could tell he wasn't himself but couldn't figure out if it was the champagne or the drugs. Like he was just so nervous or something, I couldn't figure it out and wasn't about to worry either. There was no limit to the type of drugs Jack would participate in.

I remember the first time I saw him do coke. I was shocked because he didn't seem like the type. After that first time I saw him do it, he would snort coke and pop pills all the time. Usually people who abuse drugs the way he does are violent, but he's never acted that way towards us. I liked him more when he was drunk, he would be super friendly and always gave us whatever we asked for plus more. When Jack would be high off pills and coke, he was stingy. It was a little harder trying to finesse him out of anything more than our agreed amount. That's the main reason I didn't like when he would do coke.

While Jack was sitting on the couch in the suite, he started to doze off and the more I tried to wake him up the drowsier he got. This was the type of shit I didn't have time for.

"Jack, wake up!" Normie screamed from the bed. Finally, he all of a sudden snapped out of it and jumped up like nothing was wrong. He was moving weird. We had never saw him act this way, and I was getting a strong feeling to just leave right then and there. I didn't want to upset him though and I know Normie wanted her bread for even stepping foot in that door, so did I.

"You okay baby?" I asked Jack as I started to rub his shoulders to try and calm him. He felt really tense and the way he was looking I could tell he was stressed about something. Any little noise he heard he would jump up all paranoid, I didn't like that.

Normie walked up to us trying to disguise her attitude, "Papa, we have a party to get to tonight. We hate to leave you so soon, but we're the featured dancers and we need to get our money" she told him as she started to rub her hands all over my body looking directly in his eyes, but giving me that tingling feeling I always loved.

No matter what type of dates me and Normie we went on, we were sexually attracted to each other and one touch from her could make my pussy turn into a waterfall. No other woman has ever given me that feeling she gives me, and I think that's what make our bond even stronger.

Jack got up and went over to the mini bar to pour himself a drink. Normie had me so hot already I wanted to finish what we started right then and there. She slowly caressed my breast until my bra came off, then ran her tongue over my nipples in slow motion, she knew that drove me crazy. I let out a couple soft moans and glanced at her to see she had that grin on her face. That let me know she was about to turn it up a notch.

Jack came back over to the bed with us, but instead of only his drink he had 3. "Take a shot with me ladies, it's going to be a long time before I see my favorite girls again" he said.

Normie had her face deep in my pussy I couldn't even move, let alone talk. He set the glasses down and I could tell one of them had something in it. I instantly came to my senses and popped my eyes all the way open. Normie was still kissing all over me and just when she was about to grab the shot, I accidently knocked it over on purpose. I'm not sure if he meant to put something in his own drink, but this was a big night for us, and we weren't about to take any chances for it to go wrong.

"Dynasti are you okay?" Jack said upset.
"What did you put in those drinks papa?"

I put on my sexy voice so he would calm down, because even if this situation went left, we still needed to be paid.

Jack just stood there then suddenly his eyes started to roll to the back of his head and he collapsed.

"Shit" Normie yelled, she tried to catch him, but was a little bit too late. "What the fuck did this man take, he been tweaking all night" I said as I tried not to panic. I looked around for his suitcase that he usually keeps his money in and found it under the bed. When I opened it, I couldn't believe my eyes.

What the hell was he doing with all this cash in a suitcase like this. That wasn't like him to be carrying large amounts of money around. It had to been over $100,000. I've never saw that much money at once before, and I ain't gonna lie, I was in a daze. The man is lucky we actually care about him because all that money would have been ours, period. I've always been an honest person and even though it looks like Jack just wasted our time, I wasn't going to blame him. From the looks of it, he has something serious going on in his life and he was carrying that much money in a briefcase like that, I'm sure it was for a reason.

After a few minutes of staring at all that money, I grabbed the $5,000 he owed us for the night. It was already 11pm and we needed to make it to the club asap. Jack has never been off his ass like this, so I decided to leave him a note for whenever he woke up.

*"Hey papa its D and Normie. You must have had a little too much to drink tonight because you couldn't stay up and play with us. We told you about the important party that we had to get to tonight so sorry we couldn't stay to cuddle with you until you woke up. You agreed to give us $2,500 a piece tonight because you're leaving out the country tomorrow. I took that out of the suitcase and didn't touch anything else. Call us when you wake up, so we'll know that you're safe. We love you Papa."*

I tucked him into the couch that he collapsed on, put a blanket over him and made sure he was still breathing, or at least I thought he was. We put on our clothes, touched up our makeup and made sure to leave everything the way it was before we got there. Normie was so anxious to get out of there, but I kind of wish we could have finished what we started. I would be sure she stayed at my house with me after the party.

Once we got in the car, we started to finish our bottle of Patron, put Dice latest album in rotation and started to turn up on our way to the party. When we pulled up to the parking lot it was super packed. They almost didn't want to let us in the gate until security recognized Normie's truck. She was the only one around the city with a custom burgundy Audi truck.

The party and video shoot was about to be super lit. We hurried up and got dressed into the custom outfits we had made and as always, all eyes were on us. I was sure not to give any of the girl's small talk, because I didn't want them all in my face once they saw I was control of everything.

By the time we made it on the floor the club was already packed. Soon as Dice saw us, he sent the $1,000 through cash app for me and Normie to be in his video. We picked 3 other girls to come in their section and dance with us. They had so many bottles and so many ones to throw, we were in their section the whole night. Even when we got called to the stage, Dice and his crew came up there and went crazy. They used our stage set as one of the scenes in his video too. It was nothing but good vibes the whole night. All together we left out with a little over $4,000 a piece, easy.

We were on our way to my house, drunk and just full of excitement from the party. We've never made that much in one night. The most I've ever made in one night just dancing was close to $3,000, now I just beat my own record. I knew for a fact that Dice video was going to be on World Star, and I was hype at the fact that he gave us our own cameo. I thought about calling Jack to check on him, but I figured I'd just wait until he hit one of us up first since I left him that letter. I already started thinking about what I wanted to do with my money. I had been stacking my money for months, so I was only planning on putting half of it up, then going shopping with the rest. I'm glad I didn't have any kids, so I ain't have to worry about none of the things that came with parenting. I could have all my money to myself.

"Come spend the night with me" I said in a soft sexy tone as we pulled up my crib. I really wanted her to finish what we started earlier, and I had some things I wanted to do with her too. Normie just smiled and said, "I was coming over anyway."

When we got in, we decided to take a shower together. I always loved Normies soft smooth skin, she was so perfect to me. I was the brown skinned beauty and she was the sexy yellow bone. We did a little kissing and teasing in the shower and by the time we got out it was daylight again. We were both fighting to stay woke so we just laid down and went straight to sleep. We'll finish what we started tomorrow, we were actually long overdue.

What had to been only a couple hours later, I heard big banging on my front door. I became irritated because it felt like I had just gone to sleep. Normie didn't budge, she was a heavy sleeper, so she just moved around a little in the bed. I waited a minute before I actually got up thinking whoever that was would just go away, but they started to knock and ring my doorbell even louder.

I looked outside the peep hole and saw an unfamiliar face, a bougie looking white lady. I'm blew because I just know it wasn't no Jehovah's witness knocking on my fucking door like that. I slung the door open with an attitude, "Who are you and who died?" I said. I'm sure she could tell I was annoyed and that I didn't appreciate the way she was banging on my door. She just looked at me straight in my eyes and as I was trying to read her, I could tell she had been crying.

"As a matter of fact, young lady somebody did die. My husband." She pulled out her phone and showed me a picture of Jack. I almost fell out, but I was trying my best to hold it together. I just stood there trying to wake all the way up, because clearly this was a dream. If Jack passed away, why in the hell was his wife at my front door? How did she even know where I lived? I could already tell this was about to be a crazy situation. I kept my cool and didn't show any emotion, something I was very good at. I even tried to look at the picture again and act like I didn't know him.

"I'm sorry ma'am but I don't know who that man is, he could be walking down the street and I wouldn't know a thing." I told her in a fake sincere tone, but the way she was looking I knew she could see right through me. Then I'm sure the fact my hands were shaking badly gave it away as well.

"Dyansti, please save the antics for another day. I know exactly who you are and what you're about. Can I please come in and explain to you why I'm here?" she said to me like she was irritated.

I ain't gonna lie I was shocked as fuck. This lady was not a fool so as bad as I didn't want to, I apologized and invited her in. Once she sat down, she started shaking and becoming emotional. "What the fuck" was all I could think. I woke Normie up and told her to join us in the living room.

I learned that Jacks real name was Manuel and his wife's name is Anna. She went on to explain to us that Manuel had a gambling problem, and a bit of a drug addiction. She knew about almost everything he did, even though he didn't know she knew. He owed some big-time drug dealer some money and was planning to pay off all his debts before they left for out of the country.

"This would be our way of starting over and getting a clean slate." Anna said. "That's why we're going to be gone for a whole month. I hope it's not too late. I've been doing everything I can to protect my family and now because of his irresponsible antics, there are people out here who want to harm him, and us." She sounded so hurt. I knew Jack used to party hard at times, but I would of never thought he'd be out here moving like this. I thought he was a boss.

"D, didn't you say you saw all that extra money in his suitcase" Normie said as she was still trying to process everything.

"Yeah, he had about 100k in his suitcase, and I know he doesn't carry that much cash on him like that. I took out our cut then put the suitcase back" I said to Anna. It looked like she didn't believe me, but I didn't care. I had no reason to lie.

"Are you sure it was just $100,000? Did you count it?" she asked me. I told her that I didn't, and it was really a wild guess. I noticed the money was bundled by 1,000 at a time.

"How did he die, where is his body?" Normie asked her. Then she tells us that there isn't a body, he's really missing. She knows that the people he owed money to are very powerful people in Chicago and if they took him, he's already dead.

I could not wrap my head around this situation, I'm thinking they found him dead at the hotel or something.

"With all due respect Ms. Anna, what made you come to my home?" I asked her and she seemed to get a bit irritated. No matter what she knew about her husband, ain't no way she could have found out where I lived. We don't invite the tricks to where we lay our head at.

"Dynasti, I'm actually helping you out and at the same time I need your help finding my husband's body." I looked at her like she was crazy, but I let her continue.

"Once I report him missing, the police are going to come question everybody he spoke to that day, and hopefully they don't label both of you as the number one suspects." I didn't like her tone of voice, but once again I didn't speak, I just let her talk.

"The guy he was dealing with has a lot of powerful people in his back pocket. I wouldn't be surprised if the hotel footage was already destroyed." Anna said and she was talking with a lot of attitude. This lady was starting to rub me the wrong way.

"Fuck!!" I yelled out, I could tell that I scared them both because they jumped and shot their eyes directly at me. "I left Jack a damn note before we left, you think it's still there?" I said as I started to panic. "The room is however you left it honey" Anna told us. She went on to tell us that the guys Jack was dealing with were very smart. They could of purchased a suite adjacent to his and entered that way. "Wow, what are we going to do G?" Normie said.

Anna got herself together, stood up and looked directly at me. "To my understanding you don't need any police contact the way you've been living" she said seriously. I'm just thinking to myself, "his lady has to know more about me then I think. It's crazy she said that because I'm out on bond fighting a drug trafficking case. Some shit that ain't really have nothing to do with me. I got one of the best lawyers in the city though, but I couldn't leave Illinois. If my name was in anything as far as a parking ticket, they would try to lock my ass back up. I stood up and started pacing because now I was getting nervous and next thing, I know I began to cry and scream.

"IM NOT GOING TO JAIL FOR NOBODY!!"
"We didn't do anything to him!"
"We love Jack, I would never!"
"He was my favorite fucking trick and gave us whatever we wanted!"

I couldn't control myself I started to spazz. There was no way I was stepping foot inside of

Cook County Jail again. Normie was trying her hardest to calm me down, but it wasn't working.

Anna came in front of me and said, "Listen, we have to work together. I don't care about my husband being a trick. I'm thinking about our children, our family. We're all hurting, but we have to be strong. The only thing I can tell you ladies is lay low but don't go too far."

"What if we have to go on the run? I'm a whole college student" Normie said as tears started to form in her eyes. Anna sat back down and talked about how she didn't know the names of the men who could of took Jack. I could tell she was trying to be strong, but it seemed to me she already had a feeling that this was going to happen.

"We don't know any real information about the men either, so how are we going to help" Normie said looking directly at Anna.

"I think you girls would have a better way of finding out who's behind this than me, being that you all are... ya know, escorts" she said reluctantly.

"Escorts? That's fine, I'll take it" Normie hurried up and replied to her comment before I had a chance to reply back. I needed to find out what was to this lady, because she had some nerve stepping into my house being shady.

Anna walked to the door and before leaving she mentioned that she was about to report him missing in about 4 hours since they're flight was scheduled to leave in 2. According to her, Jack was well known around the city and word would get around fast.

"I suggest you girls find somewhere to go for the day but not too far" She gave me a burner phone saying that she would call to keep me updated. Then she walked out and her driver pulled up to the curb to let her in the truck.

"We needed to find some information about this shit before we were the ones being blamed for his disappearance." That was the first thing I said to Normie once Anna left. I had a feeling that lady knew more than what she was telling us.

She was trying to act fake hurt in the beginning, but once we started to show weakness about the situation she immediately calmed down. Yeah, I'm not feeling this at all. Normie was pacing back and forth holding the phone up to her ear.

"Oh my God, Dynasti his phone keeps going to voicemail" My heart dropped again, we needed to come up with our own plan quick.

Normie and I both took a quick shower and got dressed. Even though it was Saturday, my attorney was always on call. Jordin Williamson was nothing to play with, she works at a top firm downtown and most of all she's black and she's from the hood. Knows exactly how the streets work on top of her book smarts. All the ballers in the hood hire her for their cases, and we've known each other for over 10 years. My drug trafficking case isn't the only one she's worked on for me, I have a bit of a track record. One thing about her though, is that I tell her everything and we're always upfront with each other. I texted her to meet with me asap at one of my lowkey breakfast spots in Hyde Park. She showed up within an hour.

Anytime Jordin entered a room, she would give off a confident and welcoming aura, but today I could tell she probably had a long night. She had on the baseball hat, big sunglasses combo. I've always admired her natural beauty. Usually when we meet, she'll be dressed up with her face beat to the Gods. We all ordered our food and I told her everything that was going on with Jack and his estranged wife. Jordin told us that we wouldn't be charged for his disappearance or his murder if there was no body to show up. The most the police could do was question us. I was relieved to hear that, but I still was concerned with what really happened to him.

"To be honest honey, I think the wife is into some foul play. I'm getting a weird gut feeling about her" Jordin said as she was writing in her notepad. I loved when she talked about her gut feeling, because it always reminded me of Olivia

Pope off of Scandal, and just like Olivia her gut was always right.

"I don't like her showing up to your home, you really should have called me before saying anything to her." Jordin said seriously. I explained to her that we were only running on about 3-4 hours of sleep when Jacks wife was knocking at my door, so of course my judgement was off. Then I started to think about how calm she was all of a sudden.

"That lady knows a lot about us, she even mentioned my trouble with the law" I told Jordin. What if this was all a part of some type of plan she has, those wives of super rich men be crazy sometimes.

She could have been the one that set him up to get killed and now she's trying to blame it on us to cover her tracks.

"How did she even know we were there that night?" Normie said out loud. "It's definitely something the lady ain't telling us." I replied. We told Jordin about the note I wrote, and she told us she would get some background information on them both. "We needed to find out who all had access to that room after you girls left, maybe even before. I'll do some digging"

We never cared to know Jacks real name but now I'm glad we knew it to at least try and see what all he's been up to. All I knew was that he was a powerful business owner and he used to always dress up in these fancy suits. He was one of those men who used to hang at the Soho club frequently, and you know you have to have high status to even be accepted in there. One of my homies said he's been on the waiting list for over a year.

"Did this bitch even say she went back to his suite? Or just automatically assumed all that happened" Normie was thinking out loud. I'm glad we had Jordin to help us with this situation, not sure what I'd do without her.

We all agreed to meet in a couple of days and see what the next move would be. My anxiety started kicking in and I began to shake while trying to drive. I told Normie to take the wheel, I needed to think for a minute. We sat in silence, but my thoughts were loud. It seems like we can't really trust the wife, because she's moving weird. We don't know if the money is still in the room or not, or maybe she knew where it was. My head was really spinning.

We decided we wanted to lay low, so we took a quick trip to Milwaukee. We got people out there and we needed a new scenery for at least the next day or so. Sometimes me and Normie would go to Milwaukee to work at some of their clubs, and we would support certain events. It was only like an hour and 30-minute drive from my house, so we didn't mind making that trip from time to time.

We got a room downtown at the Hilton and stopped at Benihana for dinner. I didn't want to just sit around worrying about Jack all night, so I figured we'd make a few calls and get into something while we were in town. We packed some decent outfits just in case we had to get *fine fine*.

I called my home girl Quita and told her we were about to pull up to her crib. Quita is one of my close friends, she's a bad bitch and well respected across the city. She really came from the bottom too, I watched her work her way up to the position she's in now. She owns a hair salon and a 90s themed candy store in the hood. She's always been a hustler for as long as I've known her. She had plenty money and always knew how to have a good time. Quita lives in a condo downtown so it didn't take long to get to her. "Heyyyy baby girl I missed you" she gave me a big hug. She was acting like she wanted to give me a kiss too. Quita was the first girl I ever did anything sexual with, we were so wild as teenagers. One thing I can say is that we always had a special connection since the first day we met. Even though we don't talk as much as we used to, our bond was still super tight. Quita was one of those friends that was always down for whatever. No matter how long we would go without talking, I could call her out the blue and she'll always be on go.

"I got a lot to tell you babe" I said to her. Normie and I sat at Quita's house talking, drinking and catching up. She told us she wanted us to stay with her, and we didn't need to stay at a hotel. We agreed to bring our things over there and just keep the room in case we needed it to make a few plays. "I wonder where Shaun fine ass at" Normie said. I could tell she was a little tipsy. "Call him" I told her.

Maybe his friend Tate was around. We always had fun with them, they were the type of niggas that would pay for everything for everybody no matter where we were at. I liked going to the casino with them too, I left out of Potawatomi with almost $5,000 once, and Tate only gave me $500 to play with. Of course I broke him off even though he insisted I didn't owe him anything. They would even give us money just for hanging with them for the day. They were decent tricks for sure, but they were a different breed. You know the ones that you don't really have to do anything with to get money from them, but still liked them enough to fuck around. The Milwaukee niggas got a soft spot for Chicago girls, it's just something about us.

"What's up bae, and you better have my number saved too" Normie put on her sexy voice. She chatted with Shaun for a few telling him that we were in town for the night. He told her it was their homie birthday and they were throwing him a party at the strip club. "I wonder if they'll let us work up there" I asked Normie. I already knew they was about to fuck the club up. They loved blowing bags in the strip club. I went on his Instagram story and they were on there flexing as always.

"You know what, it's cool. We don't need to work, but we'll slide up there and fuck with them." I had a sudden urge to change my mind. We would just make sure they don't spend all their money in there and link with us afterwards. No matter what I had going on, I always had money on my mind. That's why I was single, I need room to do whatever I wanted. I ain't have time for a man to be down my back all the time. I like to have my way out here.

"I hope his lil chick ain't gonna be up there." Normie said in a playful tone. She had a point though.

About a year ago it was a situation that happened with Shaun's baby mama and Normie. I tell these niggas all the time to make sure they main ladies are in check because we don't do the drama. We're always discrete with how we move, and we don't name drop or play them internet games. They really ain't have nothing to worry about on our end. It was always the niggas who wanted us to go places with them and be seen with us.

Shaun's baby mother caught him at the mall with Normie while he was cashing out on her and tried cause a scene. Once she saw my girl wasn't no punk, she calmed down. Of course, she didn't want any problems with Normie, that girl is 5'8, thick as hell and could run a mile in 10 minutes. If baby mother had kept it up, she would of got dragged for sure.

A few days after that happened, he sent Normie $3,000 just for the confusion and drama. The baby mama found Normie and would stalk her social media, but that was expected. She was a typical insecure female that was still going to be with the dude but stalk all the women he cheats on her with. She knew not to say anything to Normie though, Shaun would beat her head in like he always does. If she was at the party, she wasn't going to do shit though, so we really didn't have any worries.

I got a text from Dice asking what names we wanted him to put in the video and what our social media names were. I shot him a text right back and he told me that the video would be out in a couple days and it was going straight to Worldstar Hip-hop.com. I already knew this video was about to put us on the map and get us plenty more bookings, which was the only reason I agreed to do it in the first place. I really hope all this stuff with Jack blew over before the video drops. I was ready to get all the way in my bag and I'm not about to let nothing or nobody stop me.

We headed up to the party around 12:30. We weren't trying to be in there all night, just wanted to show our face, grab a bottle and leave. We still needed to be lowkey. As soon as we walked in the club, the first person we saw was Tate fine ass, but he had his girl with him. I was disappointed but decided to play cool.

"Look at Tate G, I thought his bitch was a little badder than that" I laughed to Normie and Quita. I wasn't hating though, if she made him happy it's all good. The type of nigga he was I thought he had a type, guess not. He ain't my nigga though, and I was still gonna fuck him if I felt like it.

We weren't dressed up like we would normally be for a club, but I didn't care. I had on a long sleeve maxi dress with my Yeezys and my diamond chain with the D on it. Normie had on a 2-piece jogging suit from Shane Justin with some Chanel gym shoes and Quita had on a Burberry shirt and shoes with some Fashion Nova jeans.

Basically we were dressed down, because I never wear gym shoes in the club.

When we approached the section that Shaun nem was at, it seemed like all the females that were with them started looking at us funny. Sometimes I like walking in their spots and being the bad bitch that nobody really knew. I wasn't feeling the vibes though, and they were actually giving us real reasons to take their men for the night.

Tate and Shaun saw us walk up and were happy to see us. They gave us all hugs and acted normal, something that I really wasn't expecting.

"Oh this was about to be easy" I thought to myself. They were about to pour us our own drinks, but we told them we already had bottles on the way. Shaun gave us all about 200 ones to throw at the strippers. We threw our money and by the time we finished our bottles we were wasted. Normie wasn't really a drinker so I knew she would be the designated driver.

As we were leaving Tate walked outside and called my name. I wasn't even worried about his lil chick that was in there with him, because he was definitely looking fine as fuck. I was tempted to make a move on him the whole night, but I ain't want to start nothing.

"Where you going, the party ain't over" he said

"We weren't staying long anyway T, what's good though" I said in a soft sexy voice.

"Come with me tonight Dynasti, I miss you"

"Oh you do huh. What about......"

As soon as I was about to bring up ole girl, he cut me off in the middle of my sentence. "That ain't my girl that's just my baby mama, I want you baby" he whispered in my ear. I was drunk and horny as fuck so what he was telling me sounded like music to my ears.

Normie was giving me that look like you good, but I knew what to expect with Tate and I wanted him just as much as he wanted me. I shared my location with them and sat inside Tate's Range Rover. He went back in the club I guess to tell his people he was leaving. I had a feeling his baby mama was going to come out trying to see what he was up to so I told Normie not to drive off until we did. I also wanted her to follow us to his crib or wherever we were going, just in case it was drama.

Tate came back to the car and drove off. I was so ready to fuck him, I started rubbing on his neck and kissing on his ear while he was driving. Next thing you know I was pulling his dick out of his pants and started sucking him just how I knew he like it. He could barely drive from the way he was swerving and moaning. I lifted my head up and figured we'll just finish this once we got back to his house.

"Bae, I know you with the shits, right?" he asked.
"What you mean baby, you know I'm always with whatever" I replied back.

That's one thing about me, the men loved me because I was a freak bitch. I was into all types of kinky shit, I did have my limits though. He didn't respond he just had a big grin on his face. I started to get a bad feeling and tried to sober up a little bit. Tate started driving super-fast, running red lights and all types of wild shit.
"Tate what the fuck" I screamed.

"Relax baby we almost there" I turned around to see if Normie was still following us, but I couldn't tell. I hadn't talked to this man in a couple of months, but I trust that he wouldn't do anything to hurt me or put me in harm's way. We've been connected for years. Even if he did hop on some bullshit, I was prepared to hold my own.

He pulled into a driveway of a house I never seen before, it looked a little too extravagant to be his house. If it was, we were about fuck all through there. There were cars parked outside and it looked like it was a party going on.

"How much you want to do the team baby?" he asked me. I was almost fully functional and couldn't believe what he just asked me. Now I know I got down and dirty sometimes for some bread, but no way I was about to go in that house and have sex with multiple men in the middle of the night. You'll never catch me on that type of time. Tate knew that shit, he used to try and finesse me some years back and I went in on him. He wanted me to fuck him and one of his friends, he never told me who the friend was though. He knew my rule, I don't deal with men that's friends or in the same circle of friends. Its either one or none. I liked to stay lowkey, and I ain't never been a pass around. I ain't care how much money a man was trying to throw at me.

"G, you got me fucked up. You should of asked me all this before we came out here"
"You were going so crazy on the dick baby, I ain't have a chance to." He shot back.

I was annoyed, horny, and real close to spazzing. He didn't seem to be too bothered about how I was reacting. It's like he already knew I was going to start tweaking on him, or he thought I would change my mind. Tate got out the car and went to the trunk to grab a duffle bag. He hopped back in the front seat and opened it enough to where I could see inside it.

"This 10k right now D, what you gonna do?"
I really couldn't believe what was happening right now. The man didn't even know I was in town until some hours ago, but now he's trying to set up a whole train. I wasn't feeling it at all. Yeah, the 10k sound good, but I'm not about to go

through extreme lengths for some cash. I could call one of my tricks right now and tell them I need $10,000, and they would have it to me within a few hours. Plus, I'm a hustler I could make 10gs in a couple days. I was still curious as to why he would come at me like that.

"How many muthafuckas in there anyway" I asked, acting like I really cared.

"It's like 6 of us all together, come on bae you know I'm about to pay you good."
"Soon as I saw you, I knew you'd be the perfect one for us tonight. We got some Milwaukee hoes in there too you ain't the only chick."

I still had a bad feeling about this, I should of just stayed my horny ass out of his way like I intended to. I started to look around to see if I recognized any of the cars even though it was dark outside. To my surprise I saw a white and orange Hellcat and knew that was nobody was Skee. I hadn't saw him in a while, but I follow him on the gram and watch his stories from time to time. I remember it was something going on with him not too long ago that went somewhat viral on Facebook. After that he went off the grid for months. He wasn't put on blast for snitching like most Milwaukee niggas though. Then I remembered, Skee got exposed for being gay and on the down low.

Crazy how after years of trying to hide it he got exposed, even though a lot of people already suspected it. So, does this mean, Tate is downlow too? I got sick to my stomach thinking about how I just swallowed his dick whole. I have nothing against gay people but being down low ain't cool to me. You can't be out here living wild like that, because men don't go to the doctor as it is after having sex with multiple women. So I knew they ain't getting checked out while having sex with men. I was disgusted.

"That's Skee car right there ain't it" I asked him. "How you know Skee?" I could already tell he was getting nervous as soon as I said the name. "I know a lot of people out here you forgot?"

Before he had a chance to reply we saw some headlights approaching us and I realized it was Normie's truck. Thank God. 10 thousand, 20 thousand it didn't matter, no way I was about to let anybody run a train on me. Especially not no gay down low ass niggas. No matter what I was into, I liked to be to be in control. I wasn't about to let this man think he could bride me to doing some wild shit. I needed to know exactly who all was in there before I even crossed the threshold.

"You know what, I'm good G, lose my number" I said as I was getting out of his truck. He tried to yank my arm, but I was too fast for him. I placed my hand inside my Louie V tote and he already knew what that meant. I always kept my strap on me.

"Okay look baby I'm sorry I'm sorry." He put his hands in the air and I was getting angrier because the man still looked so damn sexy.

"Listen, I ain't tryna do nothing to you, my people right there in that car. I'm getting the fuck out of here." I said as I looked him directly in his eyes. Before I got out and ran to Normie's truck, I made him break me off.

"I think I know what's going on here G, and if you want me to keep quiet, I'm going to need some insurance, period" I told him. He just let out a huge breath and reached in the bag, that told me everything I needed to know. He handed me $2,000 and even though I wanted more, I was ready to get far away from there, and I didn't feel like saying another word to him. That liquor wore off quick and I couldn't even believe what just happened.

After we drove off Tate tried to blow up my phone, and right when I was on the verge of blocking him, he sent me a text message.

*"Look Dynasti, I'm sorry for coming at you like that. I thought you were the ultimate hustler, I didn't expect you to take anything the wrong way. Please keep this situation between us."*

126

I didn't reply, I just couldn't face the fact that my nigga Tate was on the down low. The next morning, I called Jordin to see if she had any updates about this situation with Jack. She said she hadn't found any factual information but would be of more help when we meet Monday. I still had the burner phone Jacks' wife gave me, but she never called or texted. I reached in my bag to find the phone and noticed it was dead. "Shit" I said out loud. I never even thought to put the phone in the charger. No telling how long that phone been dead. I turned it on and saw a few messages pop up.

*"Reported him missing, cops have started full investigation"* is what the first one said.

My heart dropped, I really hope he wasn't dead for real, and I pray that me and Normie weren't going to be blamed for his death. I needed a moment to take everything in. I was ready to go back home, this trip to Milwaukee was the total opposite of what it was intended to be. Even though I came up 2 stacks, I would have rather gone without finding out about Tate. I can't lie, it hurt my feelings. He was too fine for all that, and now he's out here living foul. I hated to see it.

We left Quitas' house later that evening and checked out of our hotel room. It was about 7pm when we made it back to Chicago and we were starving. I didn't feel like sitting down to eat so Normie and I ordered us some Ruth Chris to-go. My homegirl Roxie was the manager up there and she always hooks us up.

Instead of going back to my place we went to Normie's house in Country Club Hills. I loved going to her house because it was so comfy, and she was a bomb decorator.

"I wish all of this was just a nightmare honestly" Normie said as she sat next to me on the couch. "This is a nightmare, we're just living through it" I replied back.

The next morning, I woke up to a call from Jack's wife. That burner phone had a loud annoying ringtone.

"Hello"

"Dynasti, sorry if I caught you at a bad time"

"No, it's okay I needed to get up anyway"

"Did you find any information about the guys that could have taken my husband" she asked. I'm thinking to myself like, you're the one supposed to be gathering this information. I'm just tryna make sure our names are in the clear. That's not exactly what I said though.

"Sorry Anna, we're meeting with our attorney again today to see if she has any more information" I told her.

"So you went and hired an attorney huh?"

"Was I not supposed to?" I said with an attitude
"You're right young lady, smart move"

I was getting that weird feeling again. Why would she care if I lawyered up or not, this wasn't her life on the line? She was the one who came to my home with all this shit in the first place. Truth be told, I really hate she brought this situation it to my front door.

After a few seconds she broke the silence, "Well, I did get a name"
"What's the name?"
"Darius is the first name, my source couldn't provide a last name, but they assured to me that it was Hispanic descent."
"That's a common name, do you know how many niggas in the hood who has the name Darius." I told her. I was disappointed that was all she had. Nobody around here are called by their government names anyway, not even me and Normie.
"I'll call you with n update this afternoon" I said in a hurry then rushed her off the phone. I looked at the clock and it was 8:23am, I figured I might as well stay up and get the day started.

Normie was still sleep by the time I got dressed so I decided to go downtown get us some breakfast. Right before I was about to leave Dice sent me the link to the video, we were featured in. It was fire, I loved it and the song was hot.

Everybody said this gonna be a hit that's why he wanted to drop the video and song on the same day. I went in Normie's room to wake her up and show her the video, then I stopped dead in my tracks. Dice real name was Darius and he was definitely Hispanic.

"I never knew his real name was Darius" Normie said to me as she was barely waking up. "I'm telling you G, I think its him that took Jack, too many clues add up to him" I told her as I was pacing back and forth.

This was bad and we honestly ain't got shit to do with what's going on with Jack. If his wife found out we were in cahoots with Dice, her ass would be trying to pin this on us for sure. I could tell by the way she's acting that she doesn't really care for us like that. She's acting like she doing us a favor by telling us what's going, but I bet you she has her own plan behind all of this.

I wouldn't be surprised if her ass was wearing a wire when she came to my house. I didn't know what to think. I decided to call her and try to play with her head a little bit.
"Hello, Dynasti"
"Hey Ms. Anna, I have a few questions for you" when I said that she was quick to cut me off.
"I was just about to call you, I have more information" she said in a cheerful tone. I wasn't too excited to hear what she about to say though.

"My sources are telling me that the men my husband were involved with are artists. The main guys street name is Dice. Do you know him?" she asked me. I could tell that she was being sarcastic when she asked me that, I knew it was some weird shit going on.

All I could do was drop the phone in disbelief. I hung up on Anna and told Normie to hurry up and pack her bags, we needed to get the fuck out of Chicago asap!

TO BE CONTINUED.......

# CRAZY IN LOVE

I was laying in my bed drunk, happy, confused, all of the above. Ben had just left after putting in some rounds with me. That man really knew how to satisfy me sexually, and he left me a couple thousand on my dresser like always. Now Ben was my man, but he wasn't mine. We've been messing around for a while now and it's been cool, but he has a woman and 4 kids at home. Thank God she isn't his wife, but I wouldn't know for sure if she was or wasn't. He always tells me about how his kids were nice and respectful, but their mom was a different story. Ben would come to me as an outlet to escape his reality at times.

Now I know what you're thinking, yes, I'm a side chick, but he wasn't the only man I was dealing with. I didn't see him that often either, maybe once or twice a week. We didn't only have sex we connected on a more spiritual level, and he always spoiled me and made sure I was always on my shit.

A couple of months after I met him, I found out about his hidden family at home, but before I could confront him about it his brother was killed.

When he came over to tell me about his brother's death, he told me everything about his life. I felt bad for him because of his big loss and decided to still see him. I had met his brother Jay a few times, he was really cool, and didn't deserve to go out like he did. Shortly after Jays funeral, Ben fell off bad, he had really lost his best friend. I noticed the change in him, and I helped him back on his feet. It wasn't only about money, he just wasn't the same person anymore. He wasn't healthy at all mentally, physically nor financially. He was losing out on property deals, letting people slide when it came time to collect, and he was even letting people take advantage of him. Despite his personal life choices, he was a very smart and wealthy man, all he needed was some genuine love and support. I figured his kids mother wasn't the one that was caring for him in the ways he needed to be cared for.

Once he was back and better than ever, he always told me he owed me his life. He's actually really crazy about me, I thought it was cute at first, but then things were starting to get weird. I got love for Ben, but I knew for a fact he loved me 10 times more.

After he left, I was getting up to go take a shower and my phone rang, it was him. "Dang you miss me already huh?" I said as I picked it up, but the voice I heard on the other end wasn't him, it was a police officer.

"Hi ma'am this is Officer Williams, are you related to Benjamin Rose?" My heart sank all the way down to my knees I couldn't even speak. "Are you there?" the officer said, "Yes, yes I am" I said slowly trying to pull myself together. As he began to talk everything turned into a blur as I dropped the phone then suddenly dropped to my knees. All I could remember after that was letting out a loud scream then blacking out. They needed me to come identify Bens body.

3 MONTHS EARLIER

Another day another dollar, I said to myself as my alarm clock starting ringing. It was a typical Thursday for me, one day closer to the weekend. I wasn't complaining though, because I enjoyed my job. I'm a branding manager for a top clothing company in Milwaukee, and I was working on starting my own branding company soon. I turned on my morning playlist and began to send out my good morning messages and affirmations. One to my mother, my best friend, and my cousin. I did this every morning while sending them a little motivation to get through the day.

When I got out the shower, I heard my phone go off, but I figured it was one of them writing back. When I finally picked up my phone, I seen it was my new boo Frank telling me "Good morning beautiful" I loved when a man called me beautiful. I responded back asap, and he said he would be downtown today for some business and wanted to take me out to lunch. I agreed.

Even though me and this guy name Ben were pretty much exclusive, I still talked to other men because Ben had a lot going on. It felt good talking to a regular man, and not a street nigga. That seemed to be all I attracted lately. Nothing against them, because at the end of the day I got love for Ben, but the lifestyle isn't anything I could get used to. I'd leave that to his baby mother.

Frank and I decided to meet at Capital Grille for lunch because it was right down the street from my job. I sat at the bar, ordered a glass of wine and waited for him to pull up. After about 10 minutes and no sign of him, I went ahead and ordered my food while checking my social media accounts on my phone.

I suddenly heard a deep voice say, "Hey beautiful" and when I turned around it was Ben. I was confused as hell, I thought this was a joke.

"What are you doing here Ben" but he didn't respond at first, he just had a big smile on his face and didn't answer the question.

"I was going to surprise you for lunch, but I see you already beat me here" he said in a low tone. I didn't speak I was still looking confused. "Aww you thought you was having lunch with that square ass nigga Frank, nah baby that ain't happening today."

So, as I'm looking at Ben, I thought to myself, this man is crazy. That was the first time he pulled a stunt like this, but he always joked about having me to his self. He claimed he didn't want me fucking with nobody else even though he had a whole family at home. I looked down at my phone and it was a text from Frank saying he had to cancel, because he had a flat tire that needed fixed. Was Ben behind this? I didn't even bother to ask, but I do know that this was a very weird situation.

Ben just ordered his food and acted normal as if he was the one, I was originally meeting for lunch. I took mental notes, got another glass of wine and just started to tell him about my day. We ate, talked a little bit then I left to go back to work.

I really could not phantom what had just happened, so I took an early day and decided to finish my work at home. Was Ben stalking me? What really happened to Frank? These questions were running through my head all day. What if Ben paid Frank to try to talk to me and was controlling the whole situation? He was cool but I could tell it was something void about him, but I figured he had some personal things going on. Either way I wanted to get to the bottom of this.

As time went by, I never figured out what happened that day and Ben was still being his normal self. Shortly after it seemed like every guy I met after Ben, never worked out for some odd reason. Now we had a bond, but we weren't deeply in love or anything like that. I loved him, but it's not like we would say "I love you" before ending phone calls. It was more of a what's understood doesn't have to be explained type of thing.

He just had good dick and money and that's all I really wanted from him. What else could I expect from a man that technically not available. He was fun to be around, and he always spoiled me since day 1. I thought sex was the only thing he wanted from me, but I guess his feelings began to grow deeper. He went from giving me hundreds every time we saw each other to thousands. He even bought me a 2019 Jeep Wrangler for my birthday. I wasn't stuck with the car note or anything he got the pink slip. He even put the truck in my name instead of his.

"This man is really in love with me" I thought to myself, but the feelings weren't mutual. If he was doing all of this for me, I knew his baby mother was living the good life at home with his kids. I've never been to his house, but I heard him on the phone one day giving somebody his address. I wrote it in my notes and waited a couple of days until I decided to ride pass. He lives in a big beautiful house in Royal Oak, and it was nothing less than what I expected.

After that I continued to play along with our little relationship, situation ship, whatever it was. A lot of times when men give you expensive gifts and large amounts of money, they feel like they can control you. Ben didn't seem like the type at first, all he ever said was he didn't want me talking to any other men, but I repeatedly told him that wasn't going to happen. I always let him know that I didn't belong to him and that its selfish for him to even think that. I was more of a down bitch verses being a side bitch. I let him stash money and drugs and my house from time to time until he got his new stash house up and running. He told me he could trust me and if he left it at home, his baby mother would probably take it or spend it.

Ben sold everything, weed, pills, coke and heroine. Sometimes I would dip in his stash and take weed or a pill or 2 if I was going out with my friends. I never took any of his money though.

I was at the grocery store one day and I saw this fine ass dark skinned man who looked like he lived in the gym the way his body was so fit. I think he saw me staring at him, because when we made eye contact, he let out a little laugh, I was embarrassed but then again, I was looking good. I had just got off work. and I got my hair done the day before, so it was still looking fresh.

"Hey beautiful, how you doing?" He said in a deep but sexy voice. "I'm doing good handsome" I shot right back at him. We did a little small talk then exchanged numbers and agreed to go on a date that weekend. His name was Sage.

As I was heading out of the store walking to my car, I heard somebody yell out my name. "Nicole!" I was thinking it was Sage even though I didn't see him leave the store. Just as I was about to get in my car, I saw it was Ben. He walked up to me and gave me a big hug while kissing me in my month. I broke away from him.

"Ben what the hell are you doing here" I started yelling at him. I'm not sure what was going on, but he was starting to scare me.

"Hey beautiful you not happy to see me?" he said in a sexy tone. I don't know if I was crazy for being turned on by him or if I was crazy for not getting away from him at that very moment. I didn't speak, I just stared in his eyes and tried to read his facial expressions, but I couldn't, only because in every situation like this he seemed normal.

He's never tried to harm me before or put his hands on me. I always knew that it was a side of him that I hadn't seen before so in the back of my mind I always tried to prepare myself for it.

His phone rang and he yelled out "Oh shit, I gotta go baby" and he blew me a kiss. Before he drove out of the parking lot he yelled out "Check your glove compartment bae, I'll call you later" and I instantly got so excited because I knew it was some money, and I wanted to get new furniture for my home. I was planning on asking him for the bread the next time I saw him. I so thirsty trying to open the car door I didn't even realized that Sage hopped in the backseat of the car with Ben.

I hopped in the car then proceeded to open the glove compartment and just like I expected it was a stack of cash, so I grabbed it and noticed it was a little box underneath. "This better not be what I think it is" I thought to myself, ain't no way Ben was proposing to me. I wasn't ready to get married, let alone marry his ass. When I looked up, he had already drove off. I opened the box and it was a ring inside, a big ass beautiful diamond. There was a note inside too that said:

*Beautiful,*

*You know how much I love you and appreciate you. No this is not a marriage proposal, but it is a proposal. I couldn't live with myself if I was to ever let another man have you, or even come close to you. You have helped me become a better man in so many ways I can't even name them all. I worship the ground you walk on. I know I have my situation at home, but baby she can have that house I will buy us another one. You're the one I want and the one I want to be with. At the same time, I have a lot of loose strings to take care of. This ring is for you to promise me that you're mine and that you have my back just like I have your back. If you call my phone I'm not going to answer until a couple hours. I want you to think long and hard before you accept the ring. I love you beautiful, forever.*

Tears started to roll down my face as I read the letter, the ring was so fucking beautiful. The fact of the matter is that I didn't love him how he loved me. I thought this was a fling, it's getting deeper than what it should be.

How am I supposed to trust a man that's been dealing with me while having a whole family at home? Was this man on drugs? Then he's talking about it's a proposal, but it's not. I'm only 29 I'm not ready to be tied down to nobody yet, I still have a lot more years of life ahead of me. Not to mention all this weird shit he's been doing lately.

I needed some time to think, more than a couple of hours. I blocked his number from my phone and decided not to contact him until the next day.

The next day I woke up to a knock on my door, it was Saturday and I wasn't expecting anybody. Then I dreaded opening the door, because I figured it was Ben and I wasn't ready to talk to him yet.

I looked thru the peep hole and saw a big bouquet of roses, but I couldn't see who was holding them. "Who is it?" I yelled out but the person never said anything. I went ahead and opened the door and to my surprise, it was my ex-boyfriend Zak. "Whatttt!!!" I yelled while jumping in his arms, "How did you get here?" I asked him in excitement. "I drove baby, you miss me?" He asked me with the biggest smile on his face. Z was my best friend, I met him while we were in college, shortly after we started dating.

About a year ago he caught a drug case and was sentenced to 3 years in prison. He was supposed to get more time, but we hired him one of the best attorneys out here. I didn't go and visit him often, because they shipped him all the way to a facility in Georgia. I made sure I wrote him and always answered his calls though. He never needed me to send him money, he would actually send money to me.

Out of the blue the letters and the calls stopped. I even took a road trip down to Georgia to try and visit him, but he was moved from there and the people at that prison didn't want to tell me where he was. It broke my heart, but I didn't know what he was going through. I figured he decided not to try and live a life outside and inside the joint. One thing for sure he was the love of my life and my feelings never faded.

I invited him in and we both couldn't stop smiling while looking at each other. "Babe this is a nice place, I see all your hard is paying off. I'm proud of you" He said in that sexy voice, I always loved. I wanted to enjoy this moment, but I had to ask, "Why did you stop contacting me? That really broke my heart" I asked him. "I was sad for weeks but realized that I couldn't be selfish like that because I was unaware of the things you were going through." He looked at me confused like I just had said something crazy.

"Baby I was thinking the same thing. I never stopped reaching out to you. I would call you and your phone would go straight to voicemail every time." He explained to me.

"I even had a little burner in the joint, but it never went through" he said. So as we were both trying to figure exactly what happened, the only thing I could think of was Ben. My heart dropped, that man had been being weird lately so I wouldn't be surprised if he did this. I didn't want to bring up

Ben to Zak yet, because I was just so happy that he was here.

I grabbed my iPhone and began to open it to see my block list. It was so many different numbers on there that I hadn't even seen before. I never block numbers from my phone and I always saved contact names, so it had to be Ben. I did recognize the number from the correctional facility. "Damn" was all I could say. I had to be upfront and honest with Zak.

Before he was sentenced, he made it clear to me that he wanted me to live my life, and that he didn't want me to wait on him. I still wanted to though. He always talked about how he'll see me when he gets out, and because of the love he had for me, he'd respect any decision I made.

"Is one of these the burner numbers on this list?" I handed Z my phone. "Yep that's it baby, so you blocked me huh?" he said jokily.

"'No baby, Ben did. This guy who I've been fucking with." I told him. I went on to tell him how we been kicking it heavy.

"I honestly believe the man is obsessed with me"
"I'm not even sure how he got in my phone."

If he would do something like that, I'm sure he was the one that was keeping the letters from me and keeping my letters from going out. I finally decided that I needed to leave this man alone. I explained everything to Zak, and he thought back on some weird situations as well that happened in prison.

He told me he got a couple of hate letters in the mail, but it never said who they were from and what they were for. Just basically telling him to be careful in there and don't let the wrong phone call get him killed.

It took me some time to process all of this, I knew Ben was crazy, but I hadn't even mentioned Zak to him not one time. How was this man stalking my life like this? I decided to no longer have any weird energy up in the air, especially since I didn't know exactly what Ben was up to.

I knew I wasn't going to accept the ring but if I didn't accept the ring, I knew the money flow would stop. Call me what you want, but since I've been messing around with Ben, I've grossed about an extra $5,000 a month just from him giving it to me and I wasn't prepared to let that go. I had to think of a plan, because he's not the type that would let me go that easily. I had big plans and goals for my life, and I know that Ben was the one that was going to help me.

Now I can finance myself I make good money at my current job, but I wanted to become my own boss, and it takes money to make money. I have a 3-year plan and I'm going to stick to it.

I told Zak everything, I even told him about how Ben has been acting crazy. One thing about Zak is that he was always my best friend first. I could always talk to him about anything.

I wasn't able to do that with Ben, he would listen to me talk about little things, but anytime I mentioned another man he would get upset or quickly change the subject.

We changed the subject and Zak started to tell me about his life and all the things he had going on. I missed him so much and didn't expect to see him so soon. In my head I'm thinking I should juggle the both of them because Z had my heart and I hadn't given my heart to any other nigga after him. At the same time, I couldn't just cancel what I have going on with Ben, not yet.

I didn't bring this up to Z, and he never even questioned what our relationship would be like now that he's out. Zak has always been about his money, so I know he doesn't have a paper shortage. I was so confused at that point.

Zak left and said he had to wake up early the next morning to sign the lease for his new apartment. It wasn't too far from me either. He didn't put any pressure on anything, and I loved him even more for that.

Before he left, he told me "Now that I'm out, I got your back through whatever and you can call me for anything baby, at any time, or any place." Then he gave me a kiss on my cheek before walking out the door.

I decided to run a hot bath, roll me a blunt, pour a glass of wine and just think about my next move. Before I was about to step foot into the tub, my phone rang. I really didn't feel like being bothered at the time, so I let it ring then turned it off. I didn't even bother to see who it was. I had a lot on my mind and needed some peace and quiet.

As I was relaxing in the tub letting my slow jams play, I began to sit and visualize the life I wanted. I thought about a life with Zak, owning our own businesses, raising our children, and getting the hell up out of Detroit. We used to always talk about how we wanted to move to Atlanta. I started to reminisce on all the fun times we used to have before he went away, then I thought about the not so good times we had.

About 6 months before he was sentenced, I learned that he got another female pregnant. I felt as if that was the ultimate betrayal, because even though we were on and off at times, we were still deeply in love with each other. I went into depression after finding that out, especially since she was damn near due at the time I found out. Zak's baby mama was one of those chicks from around the way that was quick to throw some pussy at him. He was young, fine and paid. We weren't married so I guess you can say I see why he did it. I wasn't perfect and I had a couple dudes on the side as well, I would of never let one of them knock me up though.

Anyway, his baby girl was about to turn 2, he showed me pictures of her, and she was beautiful. He apologized countless times to me and proved to me that he didn't love his baby mama at all, but he also found out about the baby when it was too late. He's not even the type of man who would want her to get an abortion so that really didn't matter. I began to feel disgusted all over again.

I began to think about Ben and all that he has done for me, which was way more than any other man has done for me. Was he really about to leave his baby mama and buy me a new house? If he has been with her all this time, it's obvious that's where he wants to be and to just have me on the side. I began to get a headache, and suddenly there was knocking on my door. My heart dropped because I already knew it was Ben, he had a distinct way of knocking.

"Well hello beautiful how are you" he said with a big smile on his face. I could tell he sensed my hesitation, and his smile began to fade away. I walked up to him and gave him a big hug. Despite everything going on I did miss him, and I was due time for another payday.

"I missed you daddy" I said as I started unbuckling his pants getting ready to shove all of his 9 inches into my mouth. He moaned just how I liked him to, I even did that little trick that he likes me to do.

"So I guess this means that you accept my ring" he said in between moans. Shit, I forgot all about that ring. I didn't say anything. He grabbed my ponytail and wrapped it around his wrists causing my head to jerk back, I liked that rough shit, but he was beginning to hurt me.

"Ben let go, this hurt" I cried. He pulled it tighter. "You think I'm stupid bitch, I know you had that nigga in this fucking house" I began to get really scared. Ben had never put his hands on me or been aggressive with me ever. Before I had a chance to speak, he let go of my hair and began to slap me and punch my face. I cried and tried to run from him, but I fell and then he started dragging me across the floor.

"Bitch you belong to me, where is the fucking ring?" He yelled, but I couldn't even respond. I figured he already saw it on my dresser, so he grabbed it and put it in his pocket.

"Why are you doing this me" I said in between sobs. I crawled to bathroom and tried to lock myself in there, but he just followed me. I was in so much pain, and I was so weak I just laid there drowning in my own tears.

"Did you think I was just going to let you go back to your felony ass boyfriend" he as talking in tone I hadn't heard before, he was a whole different person right now.

"He came here, I didn't even know he was released from prison. I've been living in this condo way before I even met you." I said to him. He slapped me again. That time blood rushed out of my month and I felt so undefeated.

Ben kept slapping and punching me to the point where I didn't even feel any pain no more, I became numb. No matter how much I screamed and cried for him to stop, he didn't. I covered my face trying to protect it, but I can tell I was a little too late.

"Please Benjamin can you stop, I love you. I thought you loved me too". I said slowly. Luckily for me that's when he stopped. He didn't say anything else, he just threw the ring at me and stormed out of the house.

I could not stop crying I had never been beat up like that before, no man has ever put their hands on me. I got up to go in the bathroom, and when I went in my bedroom to find my phone, it was $10,000 on my dresser. Ben left it there for me.

I woke up the next morning, and surprisingly I wasn't in any pain. I remember popping a perc before I laid down though, I guess it was still working for me. I was scared to go look at my face in the mirror. It was Sunday, but I was sure I'd have to take off of work for a few days.

I started to tear up just thinking about what Ben did to me and couldn't decide if I wanted to get the police involved or not. He blew my phone up all night to the point where I just blocked his number and turned my phone off. I was going to get my number changed asap.

I got up out of the bed dreadfully to go and see how I looked. My heart dropped when I looked in the mirror, my face was perfectly fine. I started to examine my body, and nothing was bruised or out of the normal.

"What the fuck, was that a dream" I thought to myself. Then I ran to my bedroom to try and find the $10,000 that Ben left me after he beat me up and it was nowhere to be found. I opened every drawer, flipped my bed sheets over, everything I could think of and still no luck. Wow, that was a dream this whole time. A small part of me was wishing the dream was real, just so I could have that money. I was already thinking of the ways I wanted to spend it.

So, if that was a dream, did Zak really come home yesterday? I began to get a headache. I had dreams all the time, and a lot of times they did feel real. I could of sworn I felt every punch, slap and kick. I grabbed my phone and searched for Zaks number, because I did remember him putting it in my phone. I was really hoping that part wasn't a dream. It was there. I texted him good morning, then I began to feel happy knowing that he was out that jam.

It was Sunday and those are usually my chill days, but I needed to get out of that condo before I lost my mind. While I was getting dressed, I thought about Ben and decided to give him a call. I hadn't talked to him since he gave me the ring. After that dream I had I didn't know if I wanted to accept the ring or give it back to him. That on top of the way he's been acting lately just hasn't been sitting right with my spirit.

"Heyyyy beautiful, I miss you, where are you" Ben said as soon as he answered the phone. I don't even think it rang all the way through, he must have been waiting on my call.

"Hey love I'm at home and I…." I said but he interrupted me. "Stay there baby, I'm on my way, I have a surprise for you" then he hung up the phone. More surprises, just my luck.

I continued to get dressed. I was looking good too with my Nike jogging suit and all white Nike Air Max. I had my natural hair in a ponytail, which he loved, so I know as soon as he saw me, he was going to be trying to get my clothes off. That man could not control his self when it came to me.

As I waited for him, I grabbed the ring out my drawer, along with the $2,000 he gave me with it and just started to pray. I asked God to help me make the decision then in the middle of my prayer I stopped. How am I even disrespecting God like that when Ben still has a whole family that he goes to every night. I instantly had an attitude. Then I put the ring on my finger to see how it looks and it was love at first sight. It was so beautiful, just like me.

Ben knocked on the door and I hurry up and took the ring off. I looked through the peep hole and noticed he was holding some flowers. Roses and sunflowers, my favorite. I'm guessing that's what the surprise was.

"Shit" I thought to myself as I remember Zak bought me flowers yesterday and I didn't have time for Ben to be acting crazy, so I hurried up and put the flowers in my closet. Ben greeted me with a big hug and lifted me off the ground. I can tell he missed me. We decided to go downtown for lunch and after that he took me to do some shopping. I loved when he took me shopping because there was never a spending limit with him. It was September so they were just starting to put out all of the fall styles and I got everything I wanted, I even picked some things out for Ben too.

We racked up a bill of $14,000 and he told me he still had about $8,000 in his car in case we needed more.

"It's okay baby, you've already made my day. I love you" I said before I tried to stop myself. It just slipped out. I had never told Ben I loved him before, and his eyes lit up when he heard me say it.

"I love you more beautiful, I guess that's the answer to if you're taking my ring or not" He said then I froze up. "We need to talk Ben, but let's talk at my house. Can you spend the night with me?" I asked and of course he agreed.

I was about to fuck the shit out of him for spending a bag on me today, and hopefully once I started to unbuckle his pants in the car he would forget about that damn ring until I had more time to think. Before we went back to my house we ordered take out and as we were waiting on our food I had about 4 margaritas, so I was good and tipsy.

We got back to my place and we made love all night. It was something different about this time it was so deep and passionate, better than it had ever been. How could I leave this man alone, I think I loved him for real. I didn't even try to think too hard I just enjoyed the moment.

As we laid in bed afterwards, that's when reality set in. I was hoping that Ben didn't ask about anything, I just wanted to fall asleep in his arms for the night. We both dozed off and I rolled over to Ben putting on his clothes getting ready to leave.

"I thought you were staying with me tonight babe" I said in a sleepy tone. He just kept doing what he was doing and didn't say anything. I really didn't have the energy to press him about it, so I left it alone. Then he sat on the bed and gave me this mean look while staring in my eyes.

"I love you, but I don't love you enough to be stupid" he said slowly. My heart dropped because he was giving me the same look I remembered in my dream. I was acting like I was still sleep and didn't hear him. He just shook his head, gave me a kiss on my check and left. Now I was actually glad he left, I was so scared not knowing what he was about to do next.

I know it was just a dream and Ben had never put his hands on me in real life, but that dream was really messing with my head. After he shut the door, I closed my eyes, but I couldn't sleep. I got up to take a shower and that's when I heard my phone ring. I figured it was Ben being that it was 3 in the morning and he had just left not too long ago.

"Hi ma'am this is Officer Williams, are you related to Benjamin Rose?" My heart sank all the way down to my knees I couldn't even speak.

"Are you there?" the officer said, "Yes, yes I am" I said slowly trying to pull myself together. As he began to talk everything turned into a blur as I dropped the phone then suddenly dropped to my knees. All I could remember after that was letting out a loud scream then blacking out. They needed me to come identify Bens body.

After a couple of minutes of crying and screaming I got myself together to go down to the police station. I instantly thought about Bens family wondering why they didn't call his baby mama. I was assuming she would get a call about something like this before I would. I made it down there and began to feel sick to my stomach.

"Hi, ma'am I'm the officer who called you. I saw that this was the last number dialed on the call log that's why I reached out. We found this phone with the victim but no other identification." When he said that I was confused because I could of sworn, he told me to identify Bens body.

The officer was walking me don a long hallway and continued to talk. "Someone called in about shots fired and he was deceased prior to our arrival to the scene. I'm assuming this is the victims' phone." He said.

We made it to the window and the tears just couldn't stop flowing, but I had to be strong for Ben, that's what he would want me to do. They pulled back the blanket, and I burse into more tears than I did before. I should of had someone here with me, because this is a situation I couldn't handle alone. It wasn't even Ben on the table dead, it was Zak.

TO BE CONTINUED....

# MY SISTERS HUSBAND

How could I be so stupid? I fall for this nigga tricks every time. I keep saying I'm going to leave him alone, but I just couldn't help it, I love him. We've been messing around for 2 years now and nothing has changed. He's still a liar, he's still a cheater, and he's still married. He tries to act like him, and his wife are separated, but I know more about his wife then he thinks, being that she is my blood sister. We don't have the same mother, but we have the same father who shortly died after I was born, and she was only about 2 years old.

My mother never had custody of me, because she was addicted to drugs, so I grew up in foster care. Me and my sister never formally met, but once I found out who my real father was, I searched to see if I had any siblings and she was the only one.

I found her on Facebook, and we've been keeping in touch ever since. I saw the pics of her fine ass husband, and her beautiful children and couldn't help but to be jealous. She lived the life I've always wanted. She didn't even know we stayed in the same city, I would always lie to her about where I stayed just to avoid actually meeting her in person. I was always too nervous to meet her.

One day I was at the gym working out and just my luck, I saw her fine ass husband. I was so lonely and desperate I did whatever I could to get his attention. We talked for a little while, but I never told him my real name.

So here we are 2 years later and he's still telling me the same lies. How he's gonna get a divorce and leave his wife, how he doesn't love her, and he loves me and wants to be with me. He's even been talking about how he's going to move in with me, and how I'll be the perfect stepmom to his kids, but I was actually really tired of hearing it.

So, I thought of a plan, maybe if I tell his wife/my blood sister about us, she'll leave him, and we can finally be together for real. Yep, that's what I'm going to do. We were only sisters by blood, we never grew up together and we hadn't even seen each other in person.

At that point I really didn't care about my sister. I wanted my man to be with me, and not her. About an hour after he left my house, I rolled me up a fat one and prepared to face the drama that was about to unfold. I began to smoke and gather my thoughts together when I got a text, and guess who it was from? My sister. After I read that text my heart dropped to my knees and my hands were shaking uncontrollably.

The text read:

*"I know we haven't been the close of sisters, but I feel like within these last 2 years we've grown to become best friends. I need a HUGE FAVOR! I need to come and stay with you for a couple of days. I'm having some problems with my husband. I know he's been cheating on me, so I went to get checked and my results came back positive for HIV. I'm sooo hurt sis I don't know what to do and honestly, I think he's been sleeping with men. I can't even look at him right now, sis I really need you"*

I texted her my address and she said she'll be here right away. She didn't seem surprised when she figured out I only lived about 25 minutes away from her. I didn't know what to do or what to think.

What if I'm HIV positive? Is he really gay? We hadn't been using protection either, I was scared shitless. I started crying, shaking and still trying to smoke to try to ease my mind. So many thoughts ran thru my head then I was interrupted by another text, but it was from him.

It said:

*"My wife found out about us, she went thru my phone and saw your pics and texts, so I just told her the truth. I think she copied your number down so if she calls or texts you don't respond."*

Little did he know, it was too late. My heart was racing, and my mind was definitely all over the place. I needed to get out of here, but where would I go? Fuck that I ain't no punk. This was my life and I had to handle whatever situation I put myself in. Plus I didn't know what my sister had up her sleeve, but I was going to find out.

What if he was lying, he probably just ain't want me to find out he been sucking dick behind closed doors. That would make me HIV positive too though, and if I was, I was prepared to kill him. Then I started thinking, what if my sister was lying, and this was all a part of her plan to find out where I lived. At the end of the day no matter who was lying, the truth was we were sleeping together for the past 2 years and it was nothing I could do to change that. I loved him, even if he didn't really love me. I was starting to get used to those type of relationships. Men using me just to get what they want, then once they were tired of me, they just vanished. Not even a baby could make them stay.

One hour passed by, and I hadn't heard anything from neither one of them. Lord how am I going to explain to my sister that I'm in love with her husband. It started to get dark outside and I was getting so damn agitated. Should I text her? Should I call him? I really didn't know, so I poured me a cup of my favorite wine, rolled me another blunt, and just sat there thinking about my life and all the fucked up decisions I've been making for 34 years.

All of sudden my doorbell rings, which was weird because I was sitting by the front room window and hadn't seen any cars pull up or even ride pass. I looked thru the peep hole and it was him. The married, HIV having, lying ass gay nigga that I was madly in love with.

I screamed thru the door,

"What are you doing here?"

"Just open the door baby, please". He said and just like the dumb bitch I was, I opened it.

As he was walking in, I noticed he kept his head down. I closed the door behind him, and he finally lifted his head. I saw that he had a black eye.

"What happened?" I asked

"Yo my wife went crazy after she went through my phone. She found out about you and all the oth...." he stopped in his tracks and had the ugliest look on his face.

"The what?" I screamed. At that point my blood was boiling. The others huh? I couldn't help but cry.

"Have you been fucking men too??"

"What? Hell no!! Why would you say sum stupid shit like that bitch?" He screamed.

"That's what your wife said. She said she knew you had been cheating so she went and got tested, and it came back that she was HIV positive. I'm guessing it had to been men in your phone, because she said she thinks you're on the downlow."

Once I said that his eyes got big and he started shaking. I simply told him I don't know what type of shit you two got going on, but what I do know is that I'm not trying to be a part of it.

What he said next had me ready to pull out my pistol and fuck up his other eye.

"It was only one time" he said. Now that statement really caught me off guard. I could of sworn steam was coming out of my ears.

"Aw hell naw, get your down low gay ass out of my house NOW" I said. I began to scream and cry and punch and push him towards the door, then I saw a car pull up in my driveway. It was dark so I couldn't tell what kind of car it was. I was still crying and shaking then finally my sister stepped out of the car and began to walk up.

"Fuck, it's my sister" I said out loud. "He looked out the window and turned towards me and said "That's my wife, wait a minute. Did you say sister?" he stopped in his tracks.

"Bitch you mean to tell me you're my wife's long-lost sister that she talks so much about?" he was saying everything in a low tone, but I could tell he was pissed off. I couldn't even find the right words to say at the time. Next thing I knew he was on top of me punching me all over my face. I cried and screamed then suddenly I blacked out.

I'm not sure how long I was blacked out, all I knew was that my head was spinning, and one of eyes felt closed shut. First thought that came to my head was my sister. I tried to jump up, but I felt so dizzy, so I had to move slow. Then I thought about him *(my sister's husband)* and it was all coming back to me.

I got up and started walking around, but I didn't see or hear anybody. I looked out the window and my sister's car was gone.

Was this a dream? Couldn't be the way my face feels, this was definitely real. He's never put his hands on me before, and all because he didn't know we were sisters? What difference would that make? She was still his wife, and he was still gay. Out here jeopardizing all of our lives on top of that.

I was still walking around my house looking for my phone, and once I found it I went into the bathroom. I glanced at it for a second and didn't even notice I had 5 missed calls from an unknown number. I looked in the mirror and my face was fucked up, I instantly started crying my eyes out.

From that point on I said fuck my sister, and I had something for her husband. I wasn't about to let no man put their hands on me, I don't care how mad you were. I decided to run me some bath water and put some ice on my face. I pushed my shower curtain back, and I almost had a heart attack when all I saw was my bloody sister laying in my tub looking just like me, beat up. I started screaming her name, throwing water on her face, anything I could think of to wake her up.

"Please wake up" I cried. I checked her pulse and she was still alive. After shaking her for almost 15 mins she finally woke up. I was too scared to call the ambulance, because I didn't want to draw any extra attention to my house.

"What happened? Where am I?" That was the first thing my sister said. I'm guessing she doesn't remember anything right now.

"Get up sis" I cried. "Did he do this to you?" She was trying to talk, but no words came out. I needed to get her to a hospital asap, but damn how were we going to explain this.

I lifted her out the tub, cleaned her up a little bit and cleaned my face the best way I could. I had a banging headache, so I don't know how I was going to drive us to the hospital. I tried to stay calm, but I was freaking the fuck out. I was crying, my sister was crying, God what did we do to deserve this? I couldn't believe that lying son of a bitch put his hands on me and my sister like we were some punching bags. I drank some water then gave my sister some. She was so faint, in and out and crying so badly.

Once she calmed down, she got up and looked out the window, and said "Where is my car?" My heart dropped once again. I thought this bitch didn't remember anything.

If she remembers her, she remembers driving over here, which means she remembers that I'm her sister, and that I was fucking with her husband. I instantly got scared. Not because she remembered, but because I ain't know what to expect. I was pacing back and forth trying to think of a plan then all of a sudden, a car pulls up.

"Shit!" I screamed. It was already dark, and I only had one working eye, so I couldn't tell who it was. I wasn't about to let nobody else catch me slipping again, so I went and grabbed my pistol and waited for they ass to walk up to my door.

"What are you doing?" My sister said. I told her "I'm protecting myself, and if you knew what was best, you'll sit down and let me protect you too"

Even though my sisters face looked beat up like mine, she was still so beautiful. Her pictures did her no justice because she looked better in person. We were both looking out the window, and I caught her staring at me with the nastiest look on her face, but she didn't say anything.

"Fuck, she remembers." I thought to myself, but I just played it cool. I'll deal with her later. My phone started to ring, but this definitely was not the right time for phone calls. It was that unknown number again, so I just decided to answer.

"Who the fuck is this?" I screamed. The voice sounded really familiar, it was my sister's husband. I was really hoping that was him outside so I could shoot his ass.

"Damn baby I thought you were dead, I didn't mean to fuck you up like that, but I just spazzed out" he said. I walked in the kitchen so my sister couldn't hear me, she was still at the window trying to see if that was her car outside or not.

"What do you want?" I asked him.
"Baby, I'm sorry and I love you" he said. It actually sounded like he meant it. I stayed quiet though.

"I did this for us baby so don't be mad, but if you haven't saw by now my wife's dead body is in your bathroom" he said. I couldn't believe what I was hearing.

He continued, "I didn't know where else to put her, I took her car to go get some plastic and shit to wrap her up. Either we gonna bury her or dump her somewhere. Now we can be together baby, I'm sorry for everything you are the one I really want to be with"

This nigga really had the nerve to even think I still wanted to be with his ass. I was shaking so bad. I didn't want to go upstairs just to tell him that she was still alive. I needed to see who was in my driveway.

She was conscious and to my understanding she knew exactly what was going on, she was just trying to play it off. I was trying to think of a code way to say your fuckin wife is still alive, but I couldn't. I just hung up the phone and texted him. He texted me back;

*"Well we about to kill the bitch. I'm on my way back now. Stall her"*

I couldn't believe he was really talking like this. A side of him I had never saw before. This shit was crazy. I was not about to help this man kill my sister, his wife. She has kids that need her, and even though I never met my niece and nephew I would never do that to them, or anybody. I'm not a killer, unless I needed to be. I texted him back & said, "Fuck you! I'm not killing her" then slammed my phone on the counter.

"Who was that on that on the phone" my sister asked in the most calming tone. My head popped up and I told her, "Nobody." She looked me up and down then continued to look out the window, and it seem like she either knew who that was outside, or she was expecting somebody.

"Well you are doing a lot of panicking for it to be nobody" she said. I just felt like putting my own gun to my head and ending it all. I was so scared and confused, I didn't know what to do or say, this has been one fucked up day.

"You sure that wasn't my husband sis" she said. Tears just started rolling down my face uncontrollably. She said again but louder,

"YOU SURE THAT WASNT MY HUSBAND SIS?" I looked at her in shock.

"What he say? He probably told you to kill me, didn't he?" Then I looked at her, and she had her head down. I actually felt sorry for her, all the way up until she lifted her head up and had a smirk on her face. Then finally whoever it was in the car got out and started knocking on my door like they were the fucking police. The loud knocking made me jump and my sister just laughed at me.

"You better announce who you are or get a bullet in your head" I yelled thru the door. "It's Frank open the door" I couldn't believe my ears.

"Frank" I haven't talked to him in months what was he doing at my house, I was in the middle of some serious shit right now. I didn't have time to play these games with my ex.

So, do you remember when I said I went through a lot with men just wanting to use me and once they were finished, they would leave me? Frank was the main one.

I was pregnant with his baby about 4 years ago, and it's like he turned into a whole different person once I broke the news to him. He stopped answering my calls and texts. He never checked on me to see how I was doing, and I was really in love with him at that time and would have did anything for him.

He was the perfect spouse all the way up until I told him I was pregnant. He begged me to have an abortion, but I just couldn't do it. He tried to convince me that having a baby at that time wasn't a good decision to make, the whole nine. I didn't understand why he felt that way, because he was a good father to the 2 kids he already had, so why didn't he want to have my baby?

I was so hurt that he wasn't there every step of the way for me. No doctors' appointments together, nothing. I found out I was having his baby girl and he didn't even seem excited, being that both of his other kids were boys. When I was only 6 months pregnant, I got into a bad car accident and I lost my baby. My baby girl, that was the worst day of my life and every time I think about it, I get depressed. After the accident, Frank was trying to ease his way back in once he found out I wasn't having his baby anymore, but I wasn't going. I was done with him. Fuck him and may my precious baby girl rest in peace.

The fact of the matter was, what was this man doing at my front door? I opened the door and him and his annoying ass brother bum rushed me to get in. Next thing I know I was staring down the barrel of glock 9.

"What the fuck Frank" was all I could say. I couldn't take no more crazy shit going on, I needed answers, and I needed them asap. It was too much so I raised my pistol, me and Frank were looking each other dead in the eyes and deep down I just wanted to off him, right then & there. I still had a lot of built up anger towards him and once I saw his face, all of those emotions came back.

"Frank why are you here, we don't fuck with each other, and what I do to you to deserve a gun pointed at me?" I asked him.

"I came to check on my bitch," he said. Then walked over to my sister asking if she was okay. "What happened to your face? This wasn't a part of the plan" he said with sincerity in his voice.

"Your bitch? The plan? Frank stop fucking playing with me and tell me what's going on NOW!" I screamed, but he didn't budge. He said, "You already looked fucked up right now, I would hate to have to close your other eye shut." I couldn't believe this man was really trying to check me in my own house.

"Lower your gun and sit your ass down. I'll explain everything to you" he said, but I wasn't trying to hear that.

"I'm not sitting down shit" I screamed.

"You muthafuckas better tell me what's going on NOW, or your retarded ass brother is about a catch a bullet!" I told them as I slowly eased behind him and pointed my gun at the back of his head.

"Calm your ass down okay" My sister said. "You're the one who should be listening to him and sitting your ass down. Even though you've been fucking with my husband, I'm actually trying to save your life."

That was the most I heard my sister say all day. "What does it matter sis, you fucking with Frank over here. I'm just trying to figure out the only logical explanation for this shit" I told her.

I lowered my gun then Frank lowered his. Once it seemed calm, I couldn't control my emotions. I was crying out loud, shaking, and pacing. I screamed, "What fucking plan are yall talking about?? Did you lie to me about your husband having HIV just so you could get my address? Do you even really love your husband since you fucking with this scumbag Frank?"

I kept asking question after question, not even giving them a chance to respond. Frank stood up and said "HIV positive? So that was the results of the test? Why the fuck you didn't tell me? Now I gotta go get tested" he said.

The mood in the room definitely shifted after he said that. Frank started screaming and his eyes were turning red, he was a big guy and I was scared to see what was about to happen next.

He continued yelling, "You told this bitch before you told me? I'm going to kill you and that nigga." he looked at me with rage in his eyes,

"You should of never repeated that." My sister started crying really loud and I really couldn't make out her words. This was some sick shit going on here. I said a quick prayer to God, because I was so scared to even see what the next hour or so had in store for me.

Let's do a little review so I can try to figure some shit out before I lose my mind. Okay so I guess my sister found out that I was dealing with her husband. She went through her husband's phone, and saw all types of shit he was doing. She told me that she found out she was HIV positive, at first I was questioning that information, and I still am because I don't know if that was a part of her plan or not.

Now it looks like she's been fucking with my ex Frank, but for how long? It wasn't even important though. Now what was this plan they were talking about??? I tried to calm myself down,

177

everybody just standing around with stupid looks on their face.

I finally spoke, "Can yall please tell me about this plan that's going on? Fact of the matter is that this nigga is on his way back in my sisters car talking about let's kill her" I said to everybody.

Then my sister looked at me and said, "How stupid are you really?" Once again, I was confused by her statement.

"He was never going to kill me, he plays this same role with every bitch that he's fucking on the side. This time I was tired of it and made some extra plans of my own" she said.

My eyes grew big. Then she goes to say, "I wasn't expecting the nigga to really put his hands on me, but once he told me that he really loved you. I had a comeback for his ass. I told him about me and Frank" she started to laugh, but I really didn't find anything funny.

I couldn't do anything but sit down and listen to my sister explain this twisted story. She continues. "Frank has always been my back up. I told him where I was coming just in case I needed his protection, and if he hasn't heard from me in 30 minutes to pull up and jump out on business" I guess that explains why he was knocking on my door like that. I lifted my head and looked up at her.

"Why me? Why bring all this drama to my house? We could have handled this a different way" I told her. Then she starts laughing and said, "Are you sure you're really my sister? Because you're acting so dumb right now. I came over here to save your life. All that shit about HIV and him fucking men was just a part of my plan. I figured if I told you that you would have more sympathy for me and tell me where you stayed"

I couldn't help but to just stand there and look dumb. You would think my mouth dropped all the way to the floor. I let her finish talking though.

"My husband is not who you think he is. He's a psychopath!" she said in between laughs. "Seriously I'm not even making this up, you see what he did to you? What he did to me? He doesn't know how to handle pressure and every time it's a fucked up situation going on, he loses his mind." What's crazy is that I've been dealing with this man all this time and never knew these things about him.

"I don't love him anymore, that's why I've been with Frank. Now what you two had going on I honestly don't know anything about." She told me.

My head started pounding. A psychopath? I would of never in a million years thought that about him. I was just sitting there soaking it all in, and I told my sister to finish what she was saying.

"Every time I catch him fucking with other women his first thoughts are to eliminate the problem. He doesn't care either he is a cold-blooded killer." This situation was starting to feel like a dream for real.

"When I go thru his phone to see who he's been talking to, I only do that so I can try to warn them. The first time I caught him cheating he went crazy. I was telling him about how I was leaving him and wanted to get a divorce. That same day he left and didn't come back until the next day. Begged and pleaded with me saying he was sorry so I forgave him, all the way up until I saw on the news that a missing body was found in the woods about a week later, and when they identified her n showed her picture. I knew my husband killed her."

My sister had tears in her eyes, and I really wanted to hug her at that moment, but I decided against it. She continued.

"Ever since that happened, I've been so scared of him, I knew he would never hurt me or his kids, but any man that crazy was not predictable."

My sister continues to tell me that as the years went by, it became a repeating cycle. He would cheat, she would find out, then about a week later the body was found. She decided to get in on his plans. "We would plan to kill the women, but I was really their life saver, because I would warn them once we would get by ourselves." She tells me that when she saw me in his phone, she had to get over here.

"Those other women were just sex I could tell, but you and him were damn near in a relationship, and I can tell he cared about you from his texts, so I couldn't let him kill you. We would talk about the betrayal later, I still wanted you alive."

She looked me directly in my eyes, and I couldn't stop the tears from flowing down my face. I ran over to my sister and gave her a big hug, and we both started crying. I kept telling her I was sorry, but I couldn't even finish talking, because her husband busted threw my back door with his guns pointed and yelling, "WHAT THE FUCK IS GOING ON HERE!"

Damn. I was so into what my sister was saying I forgot about how this nigga said he was on his way back to my house.

Next thing I know it looked like an old western standoff right in the middle of my living room. My sister's husband, whose name is D by the way, had a pistol in both hands, and Frank had his glock 9 in his hand. I don't know where his brother pulled his guns from, but he had 2 pistols as well. Nobody said anything they were just starring in each other's eyes. I looked over at my sister, and she looked like she wanted to say something but couldn't. I damn sure wasn't about to say anything, because I didn't want my head blew off and my pistol was all the way on the kitchen counter, nowhere near me.

After about 5 minutes of silence I figured since this was my house, I would go ahead and break the silence. Then I noticed my sister's husband D kept looking to his side but trying not to make it noticeable. If this man had more people coming to my house, somebody was definitely about to die. All of D's friends were crazy killers, and I don't know why it never dawned on me that he was just like them. He sure does play a good role.

Before I could say anything, D spoke first. "Are you the nigga that's been fucking my wife?" he looked right at Frank. My eyes got so big, I just knew this wasn't about to end well.

Frank said, "Nigga she stopped being your wife a long time ago, that paperwork don't mean shit" and then he goes to say, "She's my women now and what you gonna do about it?"

I looked at my sister and she still was loss for words. I'm thinking she better speak up before either her husband or her boyfriend wasn't going to be leaving here alive. Yeah, her husband was a liar, cheater, and possibly a down low nigga, but at that very moment I still loved him, and would be going crazy if he was the one who ended up dead.

Maybe I should just let them do me. Lord knows I didn't want to die, but I'm the one started all of this confusion. If I wasn't being so thirsty at the gym that day, I would have never got in the bed with him, I would of never been in love with him and we all wouldn't be in this situation we're in right now.

"Everybody just calm down okay?" I said. I tried to step in the middle of them, but Frank yelled out, "Bitch move, if this fag keeps looking out the corner of his eyes his ass is dead"

"NO!" I screamed.

"This ain't the way to handle this"

Then D says, "Don't call my girl no bitch." I snapped my neck fast as fuck, then looked at him like he was crazy. Now why would he say that?

"Your girl?" Frank said. Then he started laughing like he just heard the funniest joke of the year. I lowkey felt embarrassed.

Then Frank said, "I been there done that, been all up in there and hit that, so I can call her what I want." he started licking his lips just to make this man even madder. I was about to have a heart attack.

I looked at my sister and she started laughing too. There were about to make this man mad enough to kill us all.

D looked at me and said, "Is this true?" I just put my head down and said, "Yes, but this was about 3 or 4 years ago" then he screamed, "BRING YOUR ASS OVER HERE, BITCH WE BEEN FUCKIN FOR 2 YEARS SO YOU MEAN TO TELL ME I WAS AFTER THIS NIGGA?"

I was froze, I couldn't move. I didn't want to go over there by him. I didn't know what he was going to do. My face was already fucked up and I don't think it could get any worse. Then my sister yelled out "2 years?" Her smile turned into a frown really quick. I looked at her with sympathy, but I couldn't speak.

"So you mean to tell me you've been fucking my husband for 2 years? Damn, we've only been knowing each other for 2 years. Are you really my sister?? Or you just wanted to get next to my husband? Frank kill this bitch, NOW!"

I couldn't believe she said that, but truth be told I deserved it. Whatever happened, happened. All I could do was hold my head down and cry. No words came out. Then Frank's brother says, "Damn this some deep shit going on, sound like something out of a book"

I continued to cry right where I was standing, then all of a sudden, I feel the barrel of a gun against my head. It was my sister. She was acting like she really wanted to kill me.

She said, "Bitch I trusted you, I came here to save your life. Something I didn't have to do. I ain't know the betrayal ran this deep! Bitch you gonna die today"

All I could do was raise my hands in the air. I slowly turned around so I could look her in the face, but she didn't let me. Then her husband D yelled out, "Baby, put the gun down, you don't even know how to shoot. You'll mess around and hurt yourself."

"NO! If she wants to be a killer like you, then let her, I said.

"Shut the fuck up bitch" she said.

"Maybe we all should just light your ass up, you're the reason we all here in the first place"

Then Frank said, "Come on now, you might be mad right now, but I know you really don't want her dead. It's that fag ass nigga you need to be pointing the gun at"

I felt a sharp pain in my stomach, I couldn't help but to put my hands down. It was a feeling I never felt before, but I knew exactly what was going on. I couldn't say nothing. Tears started to fall down my eyes like a waterfall, please God not right now.

I didn't want this to happen in front of everybody, it was already too much going on. I just found out I was pregnant yesterday and it still hasn't become reality to me yet. I was still smoking and still drinking like I normally did. I actually just wanted it to go away, and now I was getting my wish. I was having a miscarriage right then and there. I begged my sister to please lower her gun, the pain was getting so bad I couldn't even stand up. I didn't want to collapse because that would just give them the perfect chance to do whatever they wanted to do with me.

Everybody still had their guns in the air ready for whatever so I knew any sudden noise would have bullets flying all over the place.

"Pleaseee sister" I begged. I needed to go to the bathroom right now. Blood was starting to appear threw my jogging pants, and all I heard was a big gasp from my sister. I guess she saw it first. She lowered her gun and started crying.

"Omg... are you.... were you pregnant? Are you having a miscarriage?" She slowly said thru her sobs. "Yes" was all I could say, and I looked at her husband to see his reaction. He lowered his gun looked at Frank and said, "Man I'll deal with your ass later."

Frank and his brother lowered their guns too. The whole mood in the room changed once they saw me bleeding like that. D said,

"You was pregnant? With my baby? We gotta get you to a hospital."

I screamed out "NO!"

"Yes we are, you're losing my baby right on the living room floor" he was starting to get soft.

Me and my sister started going towards the stairs to get to the bathroom. I looked back at my sister's husband and said, "It's not your baby."

"NOT MY BABY" He yelled. My sister was still helping me up the stairs. Whatever happened down there in that living room was no longer my concern. I couldn't believe I was losing another baby. I'm too old, I don't have much time left.

"Are you sure you don't need me to call an ambulance?" she asked.

"Oh God no, especially not with those crazy niggas down there" we both laughed. Then my sister says, "I'm sorry about how I was acting down there, I really snapped. It's okay if you're pregnant by D, I've already had my lawyer type up our divorce papers. I honestly cannot take being with him any longer."

I wasn't lying when I told him it wasn't his baby, truth be told I didn't know whose baby it was. It was a possibility that D could be the father, but once I did my calculations he was on a vacation with his family when I conceived.

So who is the daddy you ask? It's a pretty long story but let me make it quick before one of those fools downstairs kill each other.

About 3 or 4 years ago I was pregnant with Franks' baby. I mentioned before he dogged me through the whole pregnancy, treated me like a straight stranger.

One day I'm at the grocery store and I run into one of Franks friends name Meech. I had only been around Meech a few times, but he was the only one of Franks friends who really had his shit together. He owned laundromats, corner stores, apartment buildings, rental halls, you name it. Now I was pretty skinny back then so you could see my baby bump when I was only 4 months pregnant. I saw him at the store, and he didn't even know I was pregnant.

"Frank didn't tell you huh?" I asked Meech. Then I held my head down and said "Of course he didn't, he doesn't even want my baby. We barely talk now" Meech was beyond shocked. Like I said before, Frank takes good care of his 2 boys you would think he loved kids. Meech just had a genuine look of sympathy in his eyes and he looked like he wanted to say something, but he let me finish. Then he says, "Damn ma that's fucked up, I thought you and that nigga was good. Would of never thought he would turn on his shorty like that. But look, he's my number and if you need anything, I got you"

Now Meech had his own family, he wasn't married or anything, but he had a girlfriend and a baby.

Since that day he became like a male best friend to me. Checking on me every day, making sure I stayed healthy, all the things that I wished Frank would had been doing, and the more Meech stepped up and became my support system, the more I grew hate for Frank. I really wanted that man dead. I was getting mad all over again just thinking about it.

As weeks went by, I guess Meech told his lady about me and how Frank was doing me wrong. I really didn't have any friends, because I was always moving around. One day Meech texted me and asked me was it okay if he gave his girl my number, I told him yeah.

After time went pass, it's like they both were my best friends. We would go shopping together, pick out furniture for my baby's room, she even went to the doctor with me when I found out what I was having, and she seemed more excited than I was. I still continued to reach out to Frank, but he wasn't having it so I just said fuck him. I wonder if Meech had told him they had been kicking it with me. I was really hoping he did just so Frank would get mad.

Even after I got into that bad accident and lost my baby, Meech and his girl were there for me every step of the way. If it wasn't Meech up at the hospital with me, it was his lady there with me, then sometimes they both would be there.

I wasn't hurt that bad, just a broken arm and blunt force trauma to my abdomen area which caused me to lose my baby.

I had rarely remembered what happened that day, because I hit my head pretty hard. The doctors and police told me I was driving really fast. That was something I didn't normally do though. I was in the hospital for about 2 weeks before I went back home, and the day I was getting discharged here comes Frank walking into my room with a bouquet of flowers. I hadn't talked to him in months, and I wasn't trying to hear anything he had to say.

After I became well and back to my normal self, which took a while, Meech and his girl were still like my best friends. I hadn't been talking to Meech as much, but his girl would call me and come see me almost every day.

One night we went to a bar and got super drunk. It was these older guys in there buying us drinks left and right. We were closer to her and Meechs' house so once we left the bar, I agreed to spend the night with her, because I was still iffy about driving, and I definitely wasn't trying to drive drunk.

When we got to their house, she said Meech was out working so he probably wouldn't be in until the morning. She gave me pajamas to put on and we both got right in their king size bed. Even though I was drunk I really wasn't sleepy, so we turned on the TV and watched some old episodes of Martin. Then the drunk me really came out, I started talking about how I wasn't happy with my life and how it still bothered me how Frank did me during my pregnancy, and next thing I know I started crying.

Meechs girl, whose name is Shay by the way, just hugged me and wiped my tears away. Next thing I know we were kissing and touching all over each other. I had never been with a girl before, but from the looks of it Shay liked girls. She pulled out all types if sex toys & a strap on, she was really about that life. Shay was pretty as hell too, so I didn't even mind I just let her take advantage of me.

As time went pass she became something like my girlfriend. That one night really turned me out. Once Meech walked in one night and found out we were fucking, he didn't even seem mad. He just took off his clothes and joined in. We would have threesomes, invite other ppl and have orgies, sex parties, all types of freaky shit. It was like my hidden life that nobody knew about. So once I met D, we hit it off but the thing I had with Shay and Meech never ended.

One day not too long ago, Meech came over to my house, because he said he had to tell me something important that couldn't be told over the phone. He came to my house and broke the news to me. He seemed very upset like he wanted to kill somebody.

He said, "Yo ma that nigga Frank is foul. And yeah that's my mans, but I love you shorty. I just had to tell you"

I was scared to hear what he was about to say next. "Do you remember anything about that accident you had a while back? Please tell me you do?" he pressed me, but I didn't, I tried to put that behind me and out of my memory.

Meech says, "I just got word this nigga Frank hired somebody to cut your brake line. I guess he was salty me & Shay had been kicking it with you and he knew not to fuck with me or mine"

Wow, was all I could say. Then I fell on the floor crying historically. Meech kept telling me that nigga going to get his, but I was still upset. Meech picked me up and carried me to my room, brung me some water. I guess he couldn't help to notice how good I was looking so he agreed to lay down with me until I calmed down. This was the first time me & Meech had ever been in my room alone with each other and I know if his girl found out she would be pissed, but I couldn't help myself and neither could he.

We started kissing, touching, rubbing and even though we had done this plenty of times, it felt different. He didn't even have a condom on, but he seemed like he didn't care. We made love in my room for hours. Round after round. Then once we were done, he got dressed, kissed me on my forehead and said, "I love you shorty" I told him I loved him too. And that had to be the day I got pregnant.

Me and my sister were in my bathroom trying to get myself together she asks, "If it isn't my husband's baby then whose baby is it?"

Then I just started shaking my head and said, "Well I guess that doesn't matter anymore now does it?" She just looked at me with tears in her eyes. We finally got the bleeding to stop but the pain was unbearable.

My sister went into my room and got me a change of clothes, no matter what I definitely needed to go to the hospital. I thought about calling Meech, but it was already too much going on in my living room I just said I'll call him later.

I wanted to take a hot bath but being that my tub was full of blood I just took a quick shower in the other bathroom the best way I could. I told my sister not to go down there before I got in, but once I got out, I see she didn't listen to me.

I opened the door and I heard arguing then I heard my sister crying. Oh God I thought they would of calmed down by now. This really isn't the time.

I think I heard Frank say, "That's what we on nigga, bet you ain't know it was me in this mufucka" I'm thinking what the hell.

I yell for my sister to come back upstairs she comes to the end of the stairs and says "Sis its getting real ugly down here, what are we about to do" I didn't want to come all the way downstairs, because my stomach was still hurting bad as fuck so I went into my guess room where I keep the TV surveillance at to watch them from up here.

I took one look and almost choked on my own spit. I guess D's people finally came thru for him and these niggas were pointing guns and talking major shit. I zoomed in to see the faces and couldn't believe my eyes. One of the men standing on the side of D was Meech. Just when I thought things were going to get better, I just knew they were about to get 100 times worse. FUCK! Was all I could say.

All I know is that I'm not stepping foot downstairs. Hell no. Whatever them niggas did to each other was on them. Frank needed to be the one to end up dead, and I damn near wanna do it myself. Then I thought about how that would cause my sister a heartbreak, but if Frank and his brother did her husband that would be another heartbreak for her and her kids.

I couldn't have a crime scene in the middle of my living room. I just keep thinking like why would this nigga D call Meech. I'm pretty sure he doesn't know anything about me and Meech, because Meech wasn't the type to run his mouth. So why would he come then?? He knew this was my house, I cannot take this any longer.

I continued to watch the drama from my security cameras and saw my sister heading for the stairs. I was hoping she would bring her ass up here sooner than later.

"What's going on down there" I asked her. "It's not looking good sis, them niggas acting like they just an inch away from blowing each other's heads off."

Then she asks me, "Have you ever seen those niggas that's with D?" I know Cam, but I never even saw that other dude." She was talking about Meech.

I was trying to figure out do I tell my sister the truth about me & Meech and the bogus shit that Frank did to me? Or should I just hold off and act like I don't know anything?

"That's Meech" I said to my sister in a low tone, she replied "Meech? It sure is him, damn I guess he looks different with a black hoodie on and pistol raised in the air"

My eyes got big and I raised my head, "How you know Meech?" I couldn't believe how fucking small this city was. "Girl Meech, me & his girl Shay used to kick it back in the day. They been together since like high school. I haven't talked to him or her a while, but I guess this wouldn't be a good time for laughs and hugs"

I was relieved, I thought my sister was gonna say she fucked him too. Now I definitely was not about to play any games about Meech and Shay was my bitch too. I actually need to call her over here. She knows all about me & D so if I tell her I was having a miscarriage she wouldn't think twice about it being Meechs baby. I'm sure Meech wouldn't want her over here in the middle of all this confusion.

"How do *you* know Meech?" She caught me off guard. "Shay is my girl too and Meech that's my big homie. I always wished I could have a relationship like them. I always babysit Lil Meech for them too." I told her. Right now wasn't the time to be telling her the details of what we all had going on.

If D called Meech over here, he probably just making sure nothing happens to me. My sister gave me the side eye and she thought I didn't catch it but I did. I'm not about to tell her ass how Me,

Meech & Shay got down. Nobody really knew, but us and the other ppl that used to come to our parties. We haven't had a wild party in a while though.

Once I started messing around with D, I still fucked with Shay and Meech. I just slowed down on all that other stuff.

"Well we need to think of a plan" my sister said. "This shit done went left and I don't think them niggas gonna hold off for any longer."

I was still watching them thru my cameras, and it looks like Meech was tryna calm everything down. I wish I could hear what they were saying. That extra $75 to have sound installed would of came in handy.

"I'm not going down there" I said.

"It's the only way, this is your house and you need to take control" she told me.

"How the fuck am I going take control of anything when my pistol is down there on the counter, not to mention my stomach is still doing backflips." I snapped back at her.

As I'm looking at the cameras, all of today's events flashed thru my head. I had been sleeping with my sister's husband whose name is D. I wanted D to myself because I was lonely and didn't have a real relationship with anybody.

My sister looks thru her husband's phone and finds out me & him had been dealing. She lies and says she has HIV and her husband may be gay just to get my address, because every time he gets caught cheating, he kills the bitches. Which I really had to second guess on, if my sister said she could tell that D really cared about me versus the other chicks, why would he kill me? That doesn't make sense.

What I'm starting to think is that he really wanted to kill her. I know he fucked me up, but why would he fuck his wife up like that? Even though she says she had told him about her and Frank *(who just so happens to be my ex who I was pregnant by)* he couldn't have got that mad that quick. He had to already know about them. I'm not sure of what my sister said to her husband while I was blacked out, but I'm sure as hell was about to find out.

Now Frank and his brother came to the rescue to save my sister. D tells me that we're about to kill his wife, so I guess he calls his own backup. Cam and Meech *(the nigga who I may be pregnant by right now)* is here on D's side against Frank and his brother.

"THIS SHIT IS NOT ADDING UP" I shouted. "What do you mean" she asked.

"Exactly what it sounds like, and from this point on I ain't trusting NOBODY, not even you sis" then she stands up and says "Not even ME? Bitch you the one been fucking my husband, and possibly pregnant by him, but you don't trust me" I snapped back, "No the fuck I don't. Didn't you just have a gun to my head about 10mins ago, and it took for me to have a miscarriage right in my living room for you to have an all of a sudden change of heart?"

"We sisters by blood, not by love"and I guess that must have hit a nerve cuz she didn't even have anything to say back, which made me even more suspicious.

Then a lightbulb went off right on the top of my damn head. "I gotta question for you sis." I looked right at her face so I could see every reaction to every word I said.

"So you said you were lying about the HIV shit right" she tried to hold her head down, but I wasn't going.

"LOOK AT ME! YOU WAS LYING ABOUT THE HIV SHIT AND YO HUSBAND FUCKIN MEN RIGHT?"

So she held her head up and said "Yeah, but what you doing all that yelling for?" so I said, "That's crazy, because before you got here D came over here and I confronted him about the shit. I asked him was he gay and he said it was only one time. Why would he say that, WHY WOULD HE SAY THAT?"

I knew one thing this bitch better tell me the truth, because this is too serious to be playing around with. If D gave my sister HIV then D gave it to me, then I gave it to Meech which means Meech gave it to Shay. Then my sister probably gave it to Frank. We needed to figure it out soon.

My sister started acting like I was over here talking to myself, I really couldn't move how I wanted to because I was still in pain. If I stood up I'm pretty sure blood would start gushing down my leg.

"Okay just calm down" she said.
"I AM CALM!" Even though we both knew that was a lie.

My sister sits down herself, she says "Remember how I just told you I already had my lawyer typing up out divorce papers? Well that was the truth, I am extremely tired of my husband and the drama he brings to my front door. When I was talking to my lawyer, he was telling me that I had a good case, but not a good enough one to take from him everything I needed for me and my kids. I signed a prenup."

Then I interrupted her and said, "How do you sign a prenup for a drug dealer?" she continues to say, "I know I know, but when we first got engaged I would of signed my life over to that man. That's how much I loved him."

My sister goes on and tells me that D has a lot of money, but not as much clean money. Most of his cash is still dirty, and her lawyer told her that the Feds already had an eye on him. If they went through with the divorce, and he the feds catch up with him, they could take everything from her and the kids.

All I knew about D was that he had a lot of money stashed. Then my sister dropped a bomb on me. "My plan was to kill him, so me and kids would be straight"

"Wait a minute, wait a minute now. Your plan is to kill him huh?" I tried to keep my voice down because Lord knows I wanted to scream every word at her right now.

"Yes sis, my husband found out about me and Frank a while ago, but I kept denying it. Today is when I finally told him the truth, that's why he got so mad because I had been denying it for months."

Finally my sister is making some sense, she must have been reading my mind or something, because I was not going for that bullshit, she told me earlier.

"Continue" I pressed her.

"Me and Frank thought of this plan to kill D and frame you for it. I did find out you too were messing around I already knew how D got down."
"I think D looked in my phone and saw what me and Frank were texting about. That's probably why he called his own back up."

She started to cry and talk at the same time, "He was going to kill me, I just really can't believe it. Then he wanted you involved to help him. While he was beating on me, I played unconscious so he wouldn't really kill me right then and there, but it looks like my plan has backfired."

I honestly could not believe what I was hearing. "I'm sorry sis, I really am. Now I started some more shit and got all these extra ppl in it. I'm so sorry"

I was still lost for words, my sister was finally making sense, but I still needed some more pieces to this twisted puzzle.
"So what about the HIV shit?" I asked her.
"I don't know" she replied.
"What do you mean you don't know, it's a lot of people's lives in jeopardy right now. I need to know."

So she sits back down and started to think. "I did see a man in his phone, he always wants pics of every damn body that's how his dumb ass gets caught."

Then my sister yells out, "OH MY GOD!" She looked at me and said, "I think the nigga that was in his phone......... was Meech"

If I wasn't in so much pain I would get up and smack the shit out of my sister *(whose name is Lovely by the way)* for saying something so stupid. I loved her name, which was another reason I was so jealous of her. Her name fit her perfect and here I am with this plain jane ass name, Angel, but everybody called me Angel.

Anyway, there was nonthin she could say to convince me that Meech was gay, let alone in her husband's phone, doing what? Posing? Hell naw I wasn't going.

"So are you 100 percent sure it was Meech?" I asked her. "I think so, it really looked like him" she replied. The more she kept saying it the more I was getting mad and she could tell.

So I told her, "I think I'll have to see that for myself to believe it, Meech gets too much pussy to be fucking around with men" I really ain't mean to say that out loud though.

My sister looked at me with the side eye again and said, "So how do you know that Angel?? Let me guess, your pussy is some of the pussy he gets huh?" This bitch had a slick mouth, but I was all up for this lil game she was tryna play.

"No, but his girl Shay can get this pussy whenever she wants." I said with a smirk.

See Lovely was very conservative, I can tell she wasn't a freak like me. Her husband told me all about her. Why do you think he cheats on her? Her ass can't ride dick like I do. A look of disgust ran across her face and I just started laughing.

"Ok, well I don't know, but it sure looked like Meech to me" she tried to say in a low tone. So I had quick comeback for her, "You ain't even know Meech was standing there right in your face, but you mean to tell me ALL OF A SUDDEN you think that was him in your husbands' phone? Cut the bullshit sis and keep it straight up with me." she really ain't have much to say after that.

I turned my head back to my cameras, and these niggas were sitting down like it was a fucking kick back in my living room. How did they go from about to blow each other's heads off to sitting down like they at a tea party or something? I knew it had to be Meech that got them calm like that. See Meech was like the king of finesse, his words were so smooth and convincing this nigga could tell you the sky was green, and you would actually believe it. That's one thing I loved about him.

Me and my sister goes to the top of the stairs to try to listen to what they were saying. I was still in so much pain soon as I stood up it got worse. I would hate to be the barrier of bad news, but this little get together would have to come to an end.

I heard Meech talking, "Everybody in here are grown ass men, now D you my mans, but you can't try to off Frank for smashing ya wife. If she going for the nigga that's on her. You been smashing shorty ain't it?" Then D stood up and says, "It's more than him smashing her, this bitch ass nigga and my wife was planning on killing me." then he pulled his pistol back out, I guess he was getting mad all over again.

"Hold on hold on bruh." Meech said trying to calm him down. Then he turns to Frank and says "Frank, you one foul ass nigga you know that?"

I can tell my sister was getting scared, she started shaking bad as fuck. Meech continues, "You already know I don't fuck with your kind, you in here tryna act so tough, but me and you know the real and you ain't gonna do shit but point that gun & talk shit, you ain't got no bodies nigga."

Frank couldn't say nothing, I guess Meech was telling the truth. That was something I never knew. For as long as I've known Frank, he always played that tough Tony role.

"Guess he just an errand boy" I said to my sister while laughing. She didn't find it funny though. Then she says, "If this nigga ain't no killer, and I'm no killer, how were we gonna pull this off?"

At that point I felt bad for her. Things still weren't adding up. These people were just using me as an excuse. Meech was straight going in on Frank down there, but how did he get these niggas to calm down? When we were down there, they looked like they wanted to kill each other, now all of a sudden these niggas are sitting on my couch like it's a fucking movie night while I was up here having a miscarriage, and dealing with my confused half-sister.

I was going to figure this shit out one way or the other, because I need to get to a hospital and I'm trying to make it out of here alive.

We were still by the stairs trying to listen in on what's going on down there. Meech seems to have control of the situation. So Frank says, "You know what Meech, this is a big misunderstanding.". Then he continues, "Aye man let me holla at you outside for a minute. No guns no nothing just man to man" Wow, Frank was really a punk. All that shit he was talking, now since Meech put the nigga on blast he wants to step outside and talk to him.

I bet you he was about to go out there to apologize on the low so wont nobody know the real him. They stepped outside and closed the door.

I went back into my guess room to look at the cameras. I bet these people ain't know I got all this shit on tape. My sister Lovely said she'll stay by the stairs and try to listen on what's going. I walk into the room, look at screen and another sharp pain came from my stomach. It wasn't because of this miscarriage either. I walked back over to the stairs and said, "Lovely, I think you wanna come in here and see this shit" I couldn't believe it. Then my sister takes one look at the screen, she gasps, and her eyes get real big. She covered her mouth and said, "What the fuck?" We thought Frank was calling Meech outside, he really called her husband out there and from the looks of it they weren't trying to fight or argue. These niggas looked like they were best friends.

"Okay now this shit is creepy" my sister said. She just sat down and started crying her eyes out. "LOVELY, WHAT THE FUCK IS GOING ON HERE. WHY IS YOUR HUSBAND AND YOUR SIDE NIGGA OUTSIDE TALKING LIKE THEY JUST REUNITED OR SOMETHING?"

I looked at her, and she was still crying not being able to talk. I tried to shake her and bring her back to reality. "Sis say something. I'm confused and we don't have much time before I pass out up here" I said to her with sympathy in my voice.

We were still looking at the cameras, and they were still talking. All of a sudden it hit me what was really going on. I got on my knees right then and there and told my sister to pray with me. I said a quick prayer for me and her, because if I didn't know before, I surely knew now that somebody was about to die and I think I'm the one that's gonna have to pull the trigger.

I turned to my sister and said, "Sis, I know I'm not the smartest person in the world, but anybody can see these niggas look like they got more in common than just fucking with you" she looked up at me and said, "What do you mean?" Then I got up and said, "Franks plan wasn't to kill D and frame me for it. Franks plan was to kill you and from the looks of it, your husband is in on it."

She gets up and runs to the bathroom without saying anything. I follow behind her and she's digging thru her purse. "What are you looking for?" I asked her. She just keeps digging until she pulls out a phone. "Got it, this is Ds phone that I went thru. He always keeps 2 phones, so he probably forgot all about this one."

I thought to myself, that's why he was calling me from an unknown number. That must of been his other phone.

My sister unlocks the phone and goes thru it, her hands are shaking so bad then she says, "I was so mad about finding you in his phone I overlooked all the other stuff." Then she drops the phone and starts crying so loud I know them niggas downstairs could hear her. I picked up the phone and there it was, it wasn't no damn Meech in her husband's phone. It was Frank.

Soon as I saw that picture of Frank a rush of anger filled my whole body. I know I hadn't been the best sister to Lovely by betraying her, but this was some downright fucked up shit. If my sister was too much of a sweet person to turn up on they ass, I sure as well was about to. Fuck the pain I'm in, the bleeding stopped so I ain't have to go to the hospital right now.

I needed to handle this first. "What you wanna do sis?" I said to her. She just kept crying, I couldn't calm her down. She had to get herself together before we went down those stairs, she needed to be levelheaded, and so did I.

I looked at her and said, "Look! You need to calm down and tell me what you want me to do? You want me to put a bullet in your husband or Frank? I ain't worried about them other niggas down there."

At the moment I forgot my pistol was still downstairs. I went back in the guess room to check the cameras, Frank and D were already back in the house, back sitting down. My sister walked in and sees on the cameras that they were back in the house, so she stops crying and tries to go down there.

"Nooo, stop Lovely right now! Not yet we need a plan." I told her. "I don't have a fucking plan Angela. What kind of plan would you have if your husband and your boyfriend were some downlow fags behind your back? Huh? I didn't think so."

She starts pacing and looking all crazy.

"You need to be mad too, you are acting like you cool with the shit. D was fucking you too. What if we all got HIV or a STD or something. You asking me what I want you to do, kill they ass. Both of them!" she said. I was getting a little freaked out by how my sister was talking. I know she was mad, but she acting like she on drugs or something, which I knew she wasn't. She doesn't even drink, never smoked, perfect church girl. Besides the fact she like dick on the side.

"You know what, fuck that I'm going down there Angela, you can stay up here if you want to. You said your pistol was on the kitchen counter, right?" and she walked right down the stairs.

"What are you doing" I tried to yell out, but it was too late. Fuck it, I might as well go down there too. I didn't know what was about to happen, but I know I couldn't leave her down there by herself.

Soon as my sister hit the bottom of the stairs everybody stood up and pulled there pistols out. These niggas were really trying to play that role. I waked over to Meech and said, "What's up Big Homie, everything cool down here?" He looked me up and down and said, "What's wrong with you Ma, you don't look 100 right now, you good?" I had to get it together this wasn't even about me. "Yeah I'm good" I replied back to him. He was looking so fine too, but I needed to stay focused.

I looked on the kitchen counter and my pistol was gone. I know my sister didn't grab it that fast, so I look over at her and she's walking up to her husband. She looks at him and says, "Put the gun down baby, he not worth it. Let's just put all this behind us. I love you baby. Fuck Frank, I never loved him." D looked at her like she was crazy.

"Are you serious Lovely?" He asked her while putting his pistol back in his jeans. I was looking at my sister like she was crazy too. What was she up to? Then she continues, "Frank ain't shit but an imposter acting like a real nigga. Matter of fact. Baby pull your pistol back out and kill that nigga. He doesn't deserve to be alive let alone breathe the same air as you" Frank looked spooked, I'm talking scared as fuck even though he had his gun raised in the air. Everybody in that room knew he wasn't no shooter though.

I guess my sister knew what she was doing. Meech was tryna step in, but I pulled him back and told him this was real personal stuff that had to get handled, and to just watch on the sideline. Then D says, "You really want me to kill him baby? Is he even worth my bullets?"

That nigga ain't really wanna shoot his undercover lover. My sister stepped back from her husband and said, "You gonna do it? Or am I gonna have to do it myself? This the nigga ruined our marriage. OFF HIS ASS RIGHT NOW D" she screamed. Her husband started shaking and getting nervous, I just let my sister have the floor, I didn't say anything.

The pain in my stomach started to get worse the more I stood up, but I really didn't want Meech to know I was having a miscarriage. I'm not sure if he would know it was his baby or not, but I rather just avoid that all together.

D raised his pistol and pointed it at Frank, then turned and pointed it at me. "Lovely, it's this bitch that needs to go. She's the one who really ruined our marriage. If it wasn't for her, we wouldn't even be here right now. She needs to die."

My sister goes back over to him and says, "No! I know she betrayed me, but this is my sister, my only sister. We could work out our problems." D didn't budge. He was acting like he really was about to shoot me. I started walking closer to him and said, "Aw so you gonna shoot me? After all we been thru. Why you can't shoot Frank, Huh? Why you switching it all on me? Is it something yall need to tell us?" D's eyes got big and I wish I hadn't said that, because it look like he was about to shoot me for real.

Meech came over and said, "Aye D you need to chill, not this one. I don't care what yall had going on, but I'm not about to sit here and let you just disrespect shorty by pointing that gun at her. Chill out bruh, work this shit out with your wife" he told him. I was so mad that D actually looked like he was going to pull the trigger, so I turned to Frank and said, "Frank, big bad Frank. Can I ask you a question?" I didn't wait for him to respond.

"Why did you do that me when we were together? Why did you have somebody cut my brake line on my car so I would crash and lose my baby? What if I would of died? You just ain't give a fuck huh? Oh you thought I didn't know that. Did you think I would just forget about it?"

Frank had a stupid look on his face, then held his head down. "Yeah that's what I thought you bitch ass nigga." I yelled at him. He was the one in the room that needed to catch a bullet. I looked over at my sister and her face just looked so shocked after she heard what I said. Then she turns to her husband and says, "D kill that nigga right now before I do," then she pulls my pistol out from behind her and aims it at Frank.

Frank still had his pistol in his hand, but he sat it down and raised his hands. He looked at D and said, "Are you really gonna let this bitch shoot me?" Everybody was looking at Frank to make sure we heard him right.

Meech shook his head and said, "I need to leave this house before it get any more deep. Yo Cam let's roll. Ain't shit shaking bruh."

As Meech was walking towards the door I tried to stop him and grab his arm. Just my luck blood started gushing down again and it was a lot this time. I couldn't help but to cry out, it hurt so bad. Meech turned around and looked at me, he looked down and acted like he just saw a ghost. "You ok Ma? You bleeding like a muthafuckas, we need to get you to a hospital, come on" I couldn't even talk, but I knew I wasn't about to leave that house. "I'm good" I said as loud as I could, which wasn't that loud. "Naw baby girl, I don't even play around with nothing like that" Meech said. Then he kneels down on the floor with me and whispered in my ear, "Shorty you was pregnant? Do you think you having a miscarriage right now" I'm not sure as to why he was whispering, but I just shook my head yeah. "Was it my baby Angel? I know a while back we got pretty intense, I didn't care though because I want you to have my baby. It's okay if you losing it right now. We can always make another one."

I couldn't believe what I was hearing right now, I always wanted a baby, especially by Meech but I don't know how Shay would feel about that. I just looked up at Meech with tears in my eyes, I told him I wasn't ready to leave, I couldn't leave my sister. I just tried my best to take the pain and see what else was about to happen.

My sister came over to me in the kitchen and said, "Are you okay? It's happening again we need to go the hospital, forget these fags." D looked at her and said, "What the fuck you just say?" Lovely turned to him and cleared her throat. "I said lets go, forget these FAGS" while looking straight in their faces. My heart started racing, because I knew it was about to get ugly.

"You think I don't know D? You think I don't know Frank? My sister has cameras all around this fucking house and were watching yall fag ass when yall stepped outside. Ain't no need to try to act like yall hate each other, yall niggas probably love each other." She was talking so fast I could barely understand her. She started talking about how it was Frank in his phone too. If I wasn't in pain, I would have added my 2 cents in too.

Frank and D couldn't even say nothing. Franks brother got up and said, "Aww okay, that's why yall niggas stepped outside huh? I knew it was some fishy shit going on here, I'm gone!" He walks out the front door and leaves. I held my head up to get a good look at D's face and he was pacing back and forth looking like he was thinking.

Frank just sat back down on the couch and didn't say nothing. My sister turned to me and said, "We going to the hospital sis, come on Meech we about to help her up" So as we were getting up off the floor I looked back and said, "Yall need to get the fuck out of my house." All I could remember next was hearing a loud BOOM. D finally pulled that trigger.

Once we heard that gunshot everybody hit the floor. Meech wasn't really too scared, because he knew D wouldn't shoot him. It was only one gunshot though. My sister was the first one to get up and realized that nobody got hit. D was just standing there looking crazy, pacing the floor. Everybody got up then Meech turns to D and says, "What's your problem man? Ain't no reason for you to be shooting in the air bringing heat to shorty crib." He replies back to him and says, "Nigga shut the fuck up. I'm calling the shots right now and ain't nobody leaving this house until I say so."

Meech just shakes his head and turns to check on me. I was still in pain and hearing that gun go off made me feel like I was going to have a heart attack. I really could not take this any longer. I wanted them out of my house.

"If you really was gonna do something with that gun you would of did it already. I'm not about to beg you to leave out of MY OWN HOUSE!! This shit is over, you and your boyfriend Frank can go off and ride into the sun together. Lovely and them babies are gonna be good, I'm going to make sure of that." I was putting my foot down once and for all.

If what I said was gonna cause me to get a bullet put in my head, then so be it. Next thing I know D aimed his gun at me and was looking like he really wanted to shoot me. "Chill out bruh for real. You mad at the wrong people." Meech says to him.

Now D is pointing the gun at Meech, but the more I look at him, the more I can tell he's going crazy. I don't know what's going on inside his head but I'm sure he's embarrassed about everything that's going on, and at the end of the day, this wasn't his plan.

My sister just kept starring at her husband with a look of disgust on her face, and I know that made him feel some type of way. Frank was looking stupid too, it really wasn't much that he could say. The proof was in the pudding. My sister Lovely spoke first, "So what now, Huh? Were you really going to kill me? Your wife, the mother of your kids? Just so you and this man could be together? I'm so disappointed in you Dieonte, I really am."

We all looked at my sister like Dieonte? Nobody ever knew Ds real name and I could see why. He didn't have anything to say though, he just looked her in her eyes and started to cry.

I didn't have time for this. So I took a look at Frank and he looked like he was tryna move in on D. Something wasn't right, I could feel it. So I told Meech to help me up, and I went over there to my sister and said, "Let's go, let's just let this whole situation go." She was really hesitant at first, but we both started walking towards my back door. Out the corner of my eyes I saw Frank walk towards D and tries to take the gun out of his hand.

D wasn't trying to let the gun go so Frank gave up. Next thing I know D aimed the gun at my sister and something told me he was about to shoot so I jumped in front of her and what do I know, this nigga pulled the trigger, and it hit me in my chest a little under my shoulder. Here I was having a miscarriage and now the man I thought I loved, who just so happens to be my sister's husband shoots me when he was really trying to shoot his wife.

Me and my sister never grew up together we never even formally met. But here I was taking a bullet for a her. I deserved to die, I deserved to lose my baby. I had a fucked up life and didn't do nothing but make it worse for myself.

After I got hit everything else was a blur, I sure knew I was about to make it to the hospital now. Meech picked me up and carried me outside to his car, I think my sister was behind us I really didn't know.

Before we drove off I heard another gunshot shot and I tried to say my sisters name but when I heard her scream out, I knew she was in the car with us. Frank ran out my back door screaming and running to the car yelling out, "He killed his self he killed his self" I couldn't believe what I was hearing, I guess D felt bad about all the events that took place today, he went ahead and took his own life.

Cyniqua Maree was born and raised in Gary, IN. Creative writing has always been her passion since she was a teenager. She started off writing poetry, then music, until later discovering her talent with short stories. She plans to continue to build her career as an author and a writer, with hopes to advance into screen writing. For more information please visit www.cyniquamaree.com

Made in the USA
Monee, IL
02 December 2021

82736603R00132